IN THE BALANCE

IN THE BALANCE

Vanessa Graham

**Willimantic Library
Service Center
1216 Main Street
Willimantic, CT 06226**

Chivers Press • Thorndike Press
Bath, England • Thorndike, Maine USA

This Large Print edition is published by Chivers Press, England, and by Thorndike Press, USA.

Published in 2000 in the U.K. by arrangement with the author.

Published in 2000 in the U.S. by arrangement with Juliet Burton Literary Agency.

U.K. Hardcover ISBN 0–7540–4251–0 (Chivers Large Print)
U.K. Softcover ISBN 0–7540–4252–9 (Camden Large Print)
U.S. Softcover ISBN 0–7862–2804–0 (General Series Edition)

The text of this Large Print edition is unabridged.
Other aspects of the book may vary from the original edition.

Set in 16 pt. New Times Roman.

Printed in Great Britain on acid-free paper.

British Library Cataloguing in Publication Data available

Library of Congress Cataloging-in-Publication Data

Graham, Vanessa.
    In the balance / Vanessa Graham.
       p.   cm.
    ISBN 0–7862–2804–0 (lg. print : sc : alk. paper)
    1. Large type books.   I. Title.
  PR6056.R286 I5   2000
  813'.54—dc21   00–044697

CHAPTER ONE

As soon as we were in the car, I regretted giving in to them. The prospect of spending the next few days with Jill and David filled me with apprehension bordering on panic. I hadn't wanted to go in the first place. After all, there was nothing to be gained by running away. The empty house would still be waiting for me sooner or later, and after a few days in the noise and bustle of Jill's home, the ensuing loneliness would only be accentuated. Also, ridiculously, I still shrank from any prolonged contact with David. But Jill, confident as always of getting her own way, had overruled my halting excuses.

'Of course you must come! How could we possibly leave you here alone? This house has always given me the creeps anyway.'

'It's home,' I said reproachfully.

'Not my home any more, thank God, and now that Father's gone I'd lose no time in getting rid of it, if I were you. I was surprised the pair of you didn't move into somewhere smaller when Mother died. It would have made things much easier for you now.'

'Don't bully me, Jillie,' I'd said with a wry smile. 'It's early days yet, and I need a bit of security to hang on to.'

'Which is why you must come back with us.

1

It'll give you a breather before you have to start making this kind of decision. You've had a ghastly time these last few weeks, and you need a break.'

At the time it seemed easier to give in. I was totally exhausted, mentally and physically, and for once in my life incapable of standing up for myself. I didn't want to go, but I didn't want to stay, either. Soon, I told myself, when the shock and pain had lessened, I could face being here alone, but not yet.

'You'll love Biddleton, Christy,' Jill said now, over her shoulder. 'It's a real picture-postcard village. We've made a lot of friends already—mostly through the children, of course. Did I tell you about the fabulous school we've managed to get Timmy into? The headmaster's wonderful—really go-ahead and brimful of ideas. It's made an incredible difference to him already.'

'In other words,' put in David drily, 'he's having to work for the first time in his young life! Did Jill tell you he's developing quite a flair for art? Must be thanks to you, because neither of us can draw a stroke.'

His eyes met mine smilingly in the driving mirror and my stupid heart contracted painfully. I remembered David's smiles with every bone in my body. I wondered briefly if he had any reservations about my proposed stay with them, but dismissed the idea at once. From the moment he had first set eyes on Jill, nine long years ago, he had had no difficulty in convincing himself that our own budding relationship had consisted merely of a casual bonhomie and, in fact, less than a month later, had actually asked me whether I thought he stood any chance with my sister! In all fairness, I'm sure he hadn't the remotest idea of how I felt, nor was it his fault if nobody I had met since had measured up to him.

I sighed and closed my eyes, and immediately Father's dear face was before me, the shrewd, kindly eyes under the bushy brows, the thick silver hair. At least he wasn't in pain any more. He had been confined to a wheelchair since his first stroke six years ago, but his brain was unaffected and he had continued to be a stimulating and intelligent companion.

Achingly I remembered what he had said on Wednesday night, after the doctor had gone and we both knew there wasn't long left.

'Don't waste your life grieving over David, Christy. He wasn't right for you, if that's any consolation.'

His words had momentarily startled me out of my grief, and he'd smiled.

'I suppose you thought you'd kept it well hidden, but I knew all along. There was nothing I could do, so I held my tongue. Never mentioned it to your mother, of course, and the idea never entered her scatter-brained little head, bless her! But I'd be easier in my mind if I knew you were settled. Whatever modern ideas women have these days, they still need a man to look after them, and no one can convince me otherwise.'

I'd bent to kiss him. 'The trouble with you is you're just an old fuddy-duddy! I'm what is known as a career woman, darling, and a very successful one, I'm happy to say!'

Echoing my train of thought, Jill said suddenly, 'It's a blessing you had a job you could do at home all these years. Heaven knows what would have happened to Father if you hadn't. We certainly couldn't have had him—not with the children and everything. In any case I'm not cut out for the Florence Nightingale scene. And you were always his favourite, anyway, you could talk to him on his own wavelength.' She smiled fleetingly. '"The clever one"—remember?'

I remembered. Jill and I had always been 'the pretty one' and 'the clever one'—as though one attribute automatically cancelled out the other. How willingly I would have traded my brains for my sister's beauty—and never more than at the time she met David. My so-called cleverness had been little help to me then, nor, for that matter, in any subsequent romances. It was difficult to appear feminine and helpless when you stood five foot ten in your stockinged feet, and having been brainwashed from infancy to believe that I was reliable, efficient and

4

capable, I was pretty well stuck with it. My first romance, at sixteen, had floundered beyond recall when my escort stood staring distractedly at the puncture in his father's front wheel, and I sprang out and kindly offered to show him how to change it. I reflected gloomily that I had never really profited from that mistake.

'I think we should stop for lunch soon,' David remarked, breaking in on my painful self-analysis. 'Ginette isn't expecting us back, is she?'

'No, I thought it would make it rather late if we tried to get home for a meal. Funny to think you've never seen the house, Christy.'

I roused myself. 'Well, you haven't been there very long, have you, and with Father being unable to be left—'

'I know, but I seem to remember you were cagey about coming to see us even in Sussex. I've wished several times lately that you were nearer, and I could just drive round for a chat.'

I hoped my face didn't mirror the astonishment I felt at this remark. Unfortunately Jill and I had never been what could be called close, and usually managed to grate on each other's nerves if we were under the same roof for more than a few days. The idea of her actually missing me was one I had difficulty in accepting.

'Well, I'm here now,' I replied a little feebly. We had a leisurely lunch in Marlborough

5

and then drove on up the Roman way to Cirencester and into Cotswold country. This was my first introduction to it, and I was immediately attracted by its quiet peaceful beauty, and glad to know I had at the last moment packed my sketchbook and watercolours. The light seemed somehow to have a special quality, emphasised by the fact that behind the sunshine the sky was darkening, and a heavy rainstorm seemed likely before long.

When we had passed Cheltenham, Jill sat forward eagerly and began to point out landmarks.

'It's not far now. In a moment we turn on to the road which leads directly to Biddleton. Here we are—see this little stream? It runs right through the bottom of the village and we have to cross it by a stone bridge. In a few minutes we'll be passing Tim's school. Just along here on the right—those are the playing fields. It's the old Manor House really, where the neighbourhood squire used to live. It's even called Manor House Prep School. Look, isn't it imposing?'

Since the house was set well back from the road and partially screened by trees, I couldn't see all that much of it—just a glimpse of the lovely Cotswold stone.

'You'll have the chance to see it properly on Saturday—it's half-term, and there's an Open Day for people to look over the school and see the boys' work and everything.'

I opened my mouth to say I should probably be travelling home on Saturday, and then closed it again, not wanting to seem ungracious.

'Here's Biddleton now, and here's the little bridge we cross to turn up the High Street. The stream widens into a pond here, look, and there are ducks. Then it flows on under the road to the next village. Just glance to your right as we turn. That's the square, where the market's held every Wednesday. And that pub on the corner is what passes as our local. The farmers and older inhabitants prefer the Fleece, half-way up the High Street. Stop at the top, David, so we can look back.'

We drove slowly up the long street which sloped gently uphill between its beautiful little houses. The quality of the stone filled me with a longing to try to capture it on canvas. I found I was sitting forward as eagerly as Jill.

At the top of the hill stood a lovely old church, and the road swept round to the left, leaving it to dominate the village from its vantage point. David obediently pulled up and we all turned to stare back the way we had come. I gave a little gasp of sheer pleasure. From where we sat the street fell away more steeply than I'd realised, and the thick, prestorm sunlight lit the stone houses with an almost unearthly glow. The turn of the road was hidden from here, and the village appeared to end in the cul-de-sac of the market square with its old, beautifully proportioned buildings on three sides. Just short of it lay the stain of dark water spattered with the white of ducks, and as a backcloth emphasising the honey-gold stone, hung the lowering purple sky.

'What did I tell you?' demanded Jill triumphantly.

'It's breathtaking!'

'If you've looked your fill we'd better get on,' David remarked, 'otherwise the rain will catch us before we're home.'

He started the engine and the car moved on past the church and out on to the road beyond the village where the last few cottages straggled. We were going uphill again now, and approaching on our left a row of about a dozen large houses standing in their own gardens. They were obviously very much newer than those in the village, but since they were also built of stone they blended perfectly with their surroundings.

'Home at last!' said Jill, and the first fat drops of rain spattered wetly on the windscreen. David had turned into the driveway of the third house along, and as he stopped the car Jill tugged open the door.

'Run, Christy, before the heavens open!'

I followed her quickly across the front garden, and a moment later we were laughing breathlessly in the large, square hall as the first crack of thunder sounded overhead. One of the doors burst open and seven-year-old Mark dashed out to greet us, followed by the smiling au-pair girl.

'Ginette, this is my sister, Miss Drew. Mark, stop pulling, do, or you'll have me over! Say hello to Auntie Christy.'

David came in with the cases, the shoulders of his jacket dark with rain.

'Take them straight up and we'll show Christy her room,' Jill directed, 'and then it will be just about time to collect Tim. You'll go, won't you?'

'Yes, of course.'

We followed him up the wide staircase.

'It's a shame it's raining, because the view from your room is lovely—right down the valley behind the village to the stream and the road we came along. You can even make out the school, when you know where to look, but now that the clouds have come right down it's hopeless. Oh, Christy, I'm so glad you like it!'

She gave me an impulsive hug, and again I was aware of gratified surprise. I couldn't quite see why my approval was so important, but if this display of affection meant that future relations between us would be more harmonious than before, I was only too ready to welcome it. David had left us, and Jill perched on the window seat with her back to the streaming pane and watched me start to unpack.

9

'There's no need for you to rush home, is there? Your time's your own now.'

'There's a certain amount of work waiting to be done, but no desperate deadlines.' Until I could better gauge my reactions to being in the same house as David as well as Jill, I didn't dare commit myself to the length of my stay. 'The best thing about being freelance is that I was able to let things run down when Father took a turn for the worse. On the other hand, I can't let my contacts slide altogether or they won't bother with me again.'

'Anyway, now that you're here we'll have plenty of opportunity for a good long natter. There's—'

A tap on the door preceded David's face round it.

'Ginette says there's a cup of tea ready if you'd like it.'

Jill frowned. 'Haven't you gone for Tim yet?' she asked somewhat unnecessarily. 'I wish you'd go—I don't want him hanging about in this weather.'

David's smile faded. 'I'll go now,' he said shortly.

'Poor David!' I said lightly, to hide my embarrassment. 'Not even time for a cup of tea!'

'He'll survive,' said Jill briefly. She stood up, smoothing down her skirt. 'I'll go down and make sure Mark isn't raiding the biscuit tin, or there won't be any left by the time we get there. Come down when you're ready.'

I snapped the lid shut on my empty case, washed my hands and sat down at the dressing-table, comb in hand, staring critically at my reflection. Jill always had the effect of making me feel colourless—an enlarged, watered-down version of the same model, but really there was no point of similarity between us. She was vivid and beautiful, with her corn-gold hair and deep blue eyes, her small, perfect features and her unfairly sun-bronzed skin. Beside her I was as clumsy and awkward as a carthorse. I had what my friends kindly called an 'interesting' face, which was about the best that could be said of it. My eyes, admittedly, were large and grey, but my mouth was also large, my nostrils flared and my chin pointed. My hair, ash-blonde to the point of silver, hung straight until, on a level with my chin, it suddenly decided to turn under into a loose pageboy. The overall effect was hardly one liable to launch a thousand ships, but I was resigned to that by now. So, for better or worse, here I was—Christina Drew, spinster. Where did I go from here?

I tugged the comb impatiently through my hair. The immediate answer was clear, anyway. Down to tea!

CHAPTER TWO

The next morning all the storm clouds had disappeared and the world was as fresh and rainwashed as only England can be on a May morning. I leant from my bedroom window drinking in the wonderful view—the backs of the village houses on the left, with their colourful gardens opening on to fields and copses which fell away to the ribbon of road at the bottom of the valley and more fields and woods beyond. From immediately below me the sound of Ginette singing came through the open kitchen window, together with a delicious aroma of coffee. For the first time in almost six weeks I felt happy. Jill had been right after all to insist I come back with them, but it would be hard when the time came to tear myself away from this lovely spot.

'I have to take Mark into Gloucester to the dentist this morning,' she said over breakfast. 'It wouldn't be much fun for you—I imagine you had enough of the car yesterday. How would you like to go and have a proper look at the village? It's Market Day and there are one or two things you could get for me, if you wouldn't mind.'

'I'd be delighted. Do I walk in?'

'There's a bus stop just across the road—a bus runs hourly on the hour. You can get off at the church if you want to walk all the way down the High Street, or there's a stop half way down near the Fleece and another at the bottom just over the bridge, so you can please yourself depending on how energetic you feel. The buses back are ten past every hour.'

I booked only as far as the church—'St Barnie's', according to the driver. I was anxious to see whether the village was as lovely as it had seemed yesterday. The church itself—the Parish Church of St Barnabas, to accord it due respect—looked ancient and peaceful and one day I'd go and look round inside. For the moment the interior of any church would recall too painfully the sad service of a few days ago. I needed the warmth and sunlight of Biddleton High Street today. I was standing where David had stopped the car yesterday afternoon, with the road running down the hill away from me, and I drew a deep breath of relief. It was no less beautiful under the blue, unclouded sky than it had been in its dramatic setting when last I had seen it.

The houses clustered together in groups on either side of the road, with tall chimneys and steeply pitched roofs. Most of them at this upper end seemed to be private houses. Immediately on my right was the village school, which Mark was attending until he was old enough to join Tim and from which he had been excused this morning for his visit to the dentist. The rest of his classmates seemed to have been let loose in the field behind the school, from which came shouts and shrieks of laughter. The square at the far end of the village, deserted last night, was now filled with market stalls and a moving, colourful throng of people.

Slowly, savouring every moment, I started to walk down the street. One of the houses opening directly on the footpath had been converted into an antique shop and I stopped to examine its treasures—delicate miniatures, hand-painted plates and ivories. Perhaps I could come here at the end of my stay and choose a gift for Jill and David. But I didn't want to think of the end of my stay. I moved on, following the curve of the road. Several people passed me, women with shopping baskets, elderly men with pipes or dogs on leads. Each one surveyed me with the friendly curiosity of those to whom a new face is a novelty. Some nodded and murmured a greeting, others merely smiled. There was an air of welcome and friendliness which, in my new loneliness, was very comforting. Unwillingly I remembered the vast, empty house waiting for me in Bournemouth and my heart sank. Jill was probably right, after all. There was really nothing to keep me there— all my friends had married or moved away. If only I could live here!

It was at this psychological moment that I saw the 'For Sale' notice and stopped dead.

Right beside me, nestling back from the road and set at an angle so that it looked down the street towards the pond, was a perfect gem of a cottage, set in a trim garden whose gay flowers made splashes of bright colour against the mellow golden-grey stone. It was love at first sight. My dazed eyes came back to the board. 'Selkirk and Bannister, Estate Agents. 170, High Street, Biddleton-on-the-Water'.

I glanced at the cottage gate, but it bore no number, only the name 'Kimble's Cottage'. I hurried down the road as though a horde of prospective buyers were at my heels, and found the agents' office on the other side just short of the stone bridge. I pushed my way through the swing doors and pressed the bell on the reception desk. A girl looked up from her typewriter and came over to me.

'Can I help you?'

'Yes, please. Is it possible to look over Kimble's Cottage, up the High Street?'

'Well, it's virtually sold, I believe.'

'Oh, no!' I stared at her in dismay, the tide of disappointment which swamped me bearing no relevance to the fact that ten minutes earlier I had been unaware of the cottage's existence.

'I'm afraid so, but we have several other—'

'Just a minute, Miss Blundell.' We both turned as a tall, pleasant-looking man came out of one of the offices. 'It's Kimble's Cottage you're interested in?'

15

'Yes. I've only just seen it, but it looked so lovely—'

'It is under offer, as Miss Blundell said, but nothing is definite until the contract is signed. We still have the keys, if you'd like to see over it?'

'Oh, I would!'

He smiled at my patent eagerness. 'I'd better introduce myself. I'm Michael Bannister.'

'Christina Drew.'

'Then, Miss Drew, let's go and see what you think of the inside of the cottage.'

We went together out into the sunlit street. 'As a matter of fact,' he continued, 'it's rather a rarity and there are several people after it. The interior was gutted by fire ten years ago, so that although it looks old-world from the outside, it's fitted with all modern conveniences inside. Which, of course, adds considerably to the price.'

I said quickly, 'I don't think that would be too much of a problem. I hope to get a good price for my old house in Bournemouth.'

He took my elbow and guided me across the road. 'That wasn't what I meant, only that it might be rather more than one would expect to pay for so small a cottage—and it is very small.'

We had reached the gate. Mr Bannister pushed it open for me and followed me up the path. There was a little porch with a miniature

16

gable over it, repeating the steeply pitched roof above. He put the key in the lock and pushed open the door.

The hall was tiny and an inverted L-shape. Immediately to the right of the door was the staircase.

'One up and two down, plus the usual offices,' said Michael Bannister.

I moved away from him, opening the door on the left to find myself in a long, low room which ran the length of the cottage, from a bow-fronted bay to french windows at the back. I walked over to them to peer through the glass at the little stone terrace and the walled garden beyond. Mr Bannister stood in the doorway. He made no comment as I passed him and opened what turned out to be the kitchen door at the back of the hall. The kitchen was small, compact and completely fitted—certainly not what one would have expected on seeing the cottage from the outside. I realised just how grateful the new owner of Kimble's Cottage should be to the fire of ten years ago. Next door to the kitchen was an even smaller bathroom.

'Indoor sanitation!' said Michael Bannister in tones of mock awe, his eyes on my face. And opposite the bathroom, round the heel of the 'L', was the door to the room on the right of the hall. It also had a bay window looking out on the High Street.

I said slowly, 'It's perfect—just perfect.'

17

'You haven't seen the bedroom yet.' He led me back into the hall and up the stairs. There was only one door, to a room which, perhaps at the time of the modernisation downstairs, had been fitted into the roof space. It ran across the front of the cottage—a light, airy room whose three windows looked down to the crowded market square beyond the bridge.

'This would be my studio.'

'Studio?'

'Yes, I paint. I wouldn't need a dining room, so I'd use that as the bedroom. This would be marvellous for working in.'

He said gently, 'Miss Drew—'

I turned to face him. 'Yes, I know. Is there nothing you can do?'

'I'm not actually handling this myself, it's being looked after by my senior partner. As a matter of fact, I've been away on holiday for ten days and this came on the market while I was away. All I know is that about three different people are interested, and one of them has actually paid a deposit.'

'I suppose it was stupid of me to come and see it, when I knew that. I think I was rather hoping I mightn't like it after all.'

'We have a lot of other properties on our books which might interest you.'

'Like this?'

'Well, not quite, of course. As I said, you don't often come across one in this condition.'

'I can imagine,' I said forlornly.

'Look, come back and have a cup of coffee and I'll get out the books and see what I can find.'

I glanced at my watch. 'I really haven't time at the moment. I've some shopping still to do and I must think about getting back for lunch.'

'Where are you staying, the Shipton Court?'

'No, I'm with my sister, Mrs Langley, at The Rise.'

'Oh, I see. Well, if you're sure you can't spare the time, I'll go and see what I can dig out, and I'll phone you if I can find anything of interest. I think I know what you're looking for.'

'Actually,' I said in a burst of honesty, 'I wasn't really looking for anything. I'm only staying with Jill and David for a few days and then going back to Bournemouth. It was just that I was passing, saw the cottage—and that was that.'

'But now that the idea of living in Biddleton has occurred to you, surely it's worth while looking at something else?'

'I don't know.' I was so taken with Kimble's Cottage that I felt, childishly, that I didn't want anything else. 'You will tell me, if there's any change?'

'Of course. Would you like to see the back garden while you're here?'

We went back downstairs and out through the back door on to the little terrace. The garden was not very big, but there were several fruit trees and a high wall ensured privacy from the neighbouring cottages.

'Is that a door in the wall?'

'Yes, it leads to an access lane which runs up behind the village street. There are several garages to let—I rather think the option of one goes with the cottage. It's also a short cut to the road beyond the village and The Rise.'

'It couldn't be better, could it?'

'How long are you staying with your sister?'

'Only a few days—probably over the weekend, because she wants me to go to the school Open Day on Saturday.'

Michael Bannister smiled. 'And meet the omniscient Mr Blair? He's fast becoming one of our major tourist attractions!'

'Anyway, thank you for bothering to come and show me round.'

'It was a pleasure. Perhaps I may phone you this evening and let you know if I've found anything?'

'I'm afraid I can't remember the number.'

'I'll find it—actually I know David quite well. We play golf together.'

'Right. I must go and do this shopping—and I'll be keeping my fingers crossed!'

Jill and I lunched alone. She had dropped Mark off at school on her way back through the village.

'Did you enjoy your morning?'

'Very much.' I hesitated, and then went on to talk of my impressions of the village and the market. I decided not to mention Kimble's Cottage, rather as one is reluctant to speak of the beloved in the early stages of a love affair. It was a secret, a dream to be cherished which couldn't come true anyway. I wasn't sure how I could explain away any phone call from Michael Bannister, but I could cross that bridge when I came to it.

'How did the dentist go?' I asked, changing the subject.

'Oh, all right—just a small filling. It's a boon being able to take him during school hours—you have to wait months for a five o'clock appointment. We won't be able to do it when he goes to Manor House.'

'Why not?'

'Mr Blair is very strict about attendance. Things like dental appointments—unless it's a real emergency—are supposed to be fitted in after school or during the holidays.'

'I shouldn't have thought it would have hurt them to miss an hour or two's schooling at that age.'

'Obviously Mr Blair doesn't agree with you. It also means we can only take our holidays during August, of course, which is rather ghastly.'

'I don't know that I care for the sound of your Mr Blair,' I said reflectively. 'He seems to have delusions of grandeur.'

Jill gave me a pitying smile. 'My dear girl, they're not delusions! Anyway, you'll see for yourself on Saturday. Actually, he's rather dishy, in a remote sort of way. All the mothers worship him!'

'Apparently,' I said drily.

Jill laughed. 'Not me, silly! But I'm so grateful for what he's doing for Timmy that I'm quite prepared to put up with his more autocratic demands. It's the discipline that makes the school what it is.'

'And what is it? One of the major tourist attractions?'

She looked at me curiously. 'What made you say that?'

I remembered that I hadn't intended to mention Michael Bannister.

'Nothing. Just the impression I get.'

'Actually, people do come and see it from quite some distance away, and there's a long waiting list. We were very lucky to get the boys in at all.'

I reached for the fruit bowl. 'I'm sure you're right—I'm glad you're so pleased with it and so well settled here. It's certainly a lovely place.'

As it happened, I was forced to admit at least a portion of my interest in the cottage when I went shopping with Jill the next morning.

'Did you notice yesterday that this cottage was for sale?' she asked, stopping at the gate.

'Yes, I did, as a matter of fact.'

'Isn't it lovely?'

'It's practically sold.'

She turned to look at me. 'How do you know?'

'I—enquired at the estate agents'.'

She said, with her eyes on my face, 'You could just do with somewhere like this, couldn't you?'

'It's rather on the small side,' I said treacherously. 'Did you remember to add biscuits to your list? Mark had the last half-dozen yesterday.'

Jill made no further comment about the cottage. Michael Bannister rang that evening, but I had covered myself now.

'Sorry I didn't manage to phone last night. I've found one or two cottages that might be of interest. May I show them to you?'

'Oh—I don't really think so, thank you all the same. It was just a spur-of-the-moment thing when I saw that one.'

'Some of these are very attractive.'

'On the High Street?'

'No, but not far away.'

But I didn't want to be buried out on the outskirts somewhere. What had appealed to me was the position of Kimble's Cottage, nestling right in the heart of the village, with all the busy life going on around it. There, I would have been alone but not lonely, able to escape to the peace of the back garden or to sit at the window and watch the world go by, as the mood took me. And Kimble's was not to be mine.

'I didn't know you knew Michael,' remarked David when I returned to the sitting-room.

'I don't really. He wanted to show me some cottages round about.'

David glanced at Jill. 'Are you thinking of moving here? That would be great.'

'No, not really. It was only that I noticed one for sale in the High Street, but it's practically sold.'

'You liked that one?'

'Oh, it was only an idea, that's all. Let's forget it.'

David said hesitantly, 'Jill, don't you think—?'

Jill stood up abruptly. 'Forget it, David. You heard what she said.'

I thought miserably, 'I wish she wouldn't speak to him like that!' Several times during the last couple of days I'd been uncomfortably aware of Jill's flashes of irritation and David's uncertain acceptance of them. There was an odd expression on his face sometimes when he looked at her—a kind of baffled hurt which tore at my heart.

She went out of the room and he met my eyes with a faintly embarrassed smile.

'Don't let Jill upset you—she gets a bit tired sometimes. I'm always telling her she does too much, what with ferrying the boys to and from school, dashing into Gloucester for meetings and lunches, and heaven knows what. Not to

24

mention being one of the leading lights of the Parents' Committee at Manor House.'

'I'm surprised that Mr Blair allows such a thing as a Parents' Committee,' I remarked acidly. 'I should have thought that all they were required to do was to supply the raw material!'

David laughed and some of the strain left his face. 'I see you've got the measure of our worthy headmaster! Oh, he's a bit big for his boots, but he's every reason to be. He devotes his whole life to that school.'

'Hard on his wife, or hasn't he got one?'

'Not yet—probably no one has come up to the required standard! But it's rumoured at the Golf Club that he's going around with the daughter of one of the governors, so he's probably on to a good thing there.'

'If she'll have him.'

'She'll have him all right, given the chance. Women seem to go for the strong, forceful types, which probably explains my own lack of success!'

I said lightly, 'Now you're being modest!'

'No. Jill can twist me round her little finger, but she doesn't really thank me for it.'

'Well, I think you're wonderful!' I knew he wouldn't take the comment seriously.

'Thank you! You must come more often!' He sobered a little. 'It is doing you good, isn't it, Christy, this break? I know you didn't really want to come, but you're glad we more or less

25

made you, aren't you?'

'Yes, you were right, I did need to get away.'

'Do you really have to go back? Permanently, I mean? There's nothing to keep you down there, surely. You're welcome to stay here as long as you like.'

'That's very sweet of you, but you know Jill and I fight like cat and dog if we're over-exposed to each other! A week's quite long enough under the same roof.'

'She really has missed you lately, though,' he said with a frown. 'Several times she's remarked that she wished you were here.' He smiled. 'I admit I was surprised the first time-you'd never struck me as being particularly close and we've managed on our own fairly adequately for nine years or whatever. But just lately she's changed somehow. I don't think she's particularly happy at the moment—oh, not just because of your father, though I know she feels guilty, as I do, that you should have had to face all that alone.'

'Please, David—' I said unsteadily.

'I know, love, I'm sorry. But if you can help her—well, you know what it would mean to me.'

'I'll try.' I didn't dare ask if he was happy himself. There was certainly strain between them which I hadn't noticed before—but of course I hadn't spent so long in their company for years. Perhaps all marriages had their ups and downs—I wasn't in a position to know.

'Don't worry,' I added foolishly, and he reached across and caught my hand.

'Bless you, Christy. You're a good friend to have—you always were.'

I couldn't look at him, but the turmoil inside me as I gently extricated my hand from his emphasised the fact that I certainly couldn't stay in this house much beyond the weekend.

CHAPTER THREE

Saturday morning dawned bright and sunny, and Tim was in a fever of excitement. I was surprised to learn that he went to school on Saturdays, only arriving home mid-afternoon. Today, of course, he would wait for us there.

'Look out for my models, won't you, Dad? There are quite a few round the classroom. And we've all got pictures up in the art wing.' That was for my benefit.

'I'm glad to hear you're interested in painting, Tim.'

'I like doing patterns and things.'

'I'll look forward to seeing them.'

At two o'clock we drove through the gateway of Manor House, Jill, David, Mark and I. By this time I had built up quite a formidable mental picture of the self-opinionated Mr Blair, and I was curious to see how near to the truth it was. I awaited his appearance on the Hall platform with interest, and I was not disappointed.

'Dishy in a remote kind of way,' Jill had said, and I saw what she meant. He was younger than I'd expected, tall and dark, with a lean clever face and a latent air of assured authority which the black gown hanging from his shoulders accentuated. He spoke lucidly and well, in a pleasantly modulated voice which carried perfectly to the farthest corner of the hall. Jill was right, he was certainly someone to be reckoned with. He made only a brief speech of welcome, and a few minutes later we left the hall and separated into groups to look at different parts of the school.

'Let's start with Tim's classroom,' Jill said, leading the way up a wide, handsome staircase. I noticed that the walls were all beautifully panelled and the balustrades intricately carved.

'I wouldn't care to turn a hundred-odd young hooligans loose in a place like this!' I remarked.

'They're hardly "let loose",' David corrected me. 'In fact, I sometimes feel the discipline tends to be over-strict for their age.'

'Nonsense, it's just what they need!' Jill contradicted. David gave me a surreptitious wink. She would obviously brook no criticism of the school.

We were lucky enough to be the first to reach Tim's classroom, and his form-master came forward to greet us. He also was younger than I had expected—perhaps I was getting old!—attractive, undeniably, but, I felt, over-conscious of the fact.

'Good afternoon, Mrs Langley—good afternoon, sir.'

'Mr Fenton, this is my sister, Miss Drew.'

He took my hand, his eyes frankly appraising, though his manner was formal enough. 'The artist? I'm delighted to meet you.'

'Oh, come now!' I demurred, 'I'm not as famous as all that! Jill must have been briefing you!'

He smiled, revealing even white teeth. 'She did mention it, when Langley first began to show signs of a leaning in that direction, but since then I've noticed your name several times—"Design by Christina Drew".'

'Well, that's very gratifying! I—'

'Come along, Christy,' Jill interrupted tartly, 'this is hardly the time or place for a summary of your career, and there are other people waiting to see Mr Fenton.'

Hot words of justification rushed to my lips, but David took my arm and squeezed it warningly as he led me over to the books laid out on the desks. 'Count to ten!' he murmured in an undertone. 'It's easier in the long run.'

'But it was so unfair! I only—'

'I know, I know. Jill, bless her, can't bear to take a back seat, even for a couple of minutes. I'm sorry she embarrassed you.'

Jill, who had stalked ahead of us, turned impatiently and waited for our approach. There were spots of bright colour on her cheeks and her eyes were brilliant. She had never looked lovelier and I had never appreciated her less. Obviously our time of compatibility was fast running out. It was perhaps fortunate that Tim joined us at that moment, making unguarded conversation out of the question. He took us on a tour round the classroom walls, pointing out with pride his own contributions, and it took me all my time to make the appropriate noises of appreciation.

'Shall we go to the studio now?' he enquired eagerly, when we had worked our way round to the door again.

I'm not quite sure what I had expected of the art display, but in any case I was in a thoroughly bad temper now and the artistic offerings round the wall seemed to my jaundiced eye singularly devoid of promise. For Tim's sake I murmured the platitudes that were required of me, but how convincing they sounded I didn't much care. I'd had enough of this school.

Jill moved down to the far end of the room with the two boys, while David and I waited, less than enthusiastically, just inside the doorway.

'What do you really think of them, Christy?'

I hesitated.

'Be honest, now.'

I met his eye squarely. 'All right, to be honest they depress me unutterably. There's not a spark of individuality anywhere—the boys might have been brainwashed. A class of chimpanzees with a paintbox would show more originality!'

He made some kind of movement with his

31

hand, but now that I had started there was no stopping me.

'I must say after all I've heard about the almighty Mr Blair I expected better than this. Perhaps he's so all-fired keen on discipline that he stamps out any spark of self-expression before it can bear fruit!'

I paused for breath, and at last something in David's face got through to me. I spun round to find to my horror that 'the almighty Mr Blair' and a party of school governors had come in and were standing just behind me. There was a jagged silence, then David made a heroic effort.

'Mr Blair, may I introduce my sister-in-law, Christina Drew?'

Somehow I dragged my eyes up—and despite my own height, it was a considerable way up—to meet the grey eyes which bored into mine. Although his face was expressionless, I knew that he was very, very angry. I could hardly blame him.

'A connoisseur of art, I presume?' he asked pleasantly.

David said loyally, 'She is an artist, yes.'

'Commercial?'

That brought my head up fully. 'I'm a graphic designer, actually.' It was no use beating about the bush. 'I need hardly say I'm sorry you happened to overhear my remarks— I had no idea you were there.'

'Obviously.'

My anger flared to meet his, but more heatedly. 'Nevertheless, I'm afraid I can't alter my opinion, which is that all these pictures—' my hand swept the room behind me '—are extremely *dull*!'

Jill, aware by this time of the fracas, had come over to join us.

Mr Blair's eyes finally left mine to rest on her. 'Good afternoon, Mrs Langley. We've been fortunate enough to hear some of your sister's views on the boys' art.'

'It's very good, isn't it?' Jill said uncertainly, aware of the tension but not the reason for it. The small group of governors shuffled their feet and one of them cleared his throat nervously.

'If you'll excuse us,' David said firmly, taking my arm, 'I think we'll move on to the science lab now. Come along, Jill, we've finished here.'

Mr Blair inclined his head slightly and moved to one side. I didn't look at any of them. In a moment we were all out in the passage. David gave a low whistle.

'Ye gods and little fishes! Sorry, Christy, that was my fault—I certainly landed you in it there!'

'Whatever was going on?' Jill demanded. David shook his head and gestured towards the boys.

'Later.'

She glanced at him impatiently, then took

hold of her sons' hands and led the way to the science wing.

'Survive the skirmish?' David enquired.

'Just about. It won't rebound on Tim, will it?'

'No, he's too fair for that. A purely personal vendetta, I would say. But oh, boy, that must have been a new experience for him!'

'Let's hope it was a salutary one!' I said, but the word 'vendetta' had disturbed me. Mr Blair was not one whom I would willingly have antagonised. Still, it was unlikely that I should see him again.

There, however, I was wrong. That evening David suggested that we should drive down to the Falcon for a drink. Apparently on Saturdays it was a generally accepted meeting place, and he and Jill usually went down. Also, the atmosphere at home since Jill had learnt of my contretemps that afternoon had been less than cordial, and a little outside companionship would certainly not go amiss. But as luck would have it, the first person I saw, as I followed Jill into the large, pleasant room, was Mr Blair. If David had not been directly behind me, I would almost certainly have beat a hasty retreat, but it was already too late. The dark head had turned, the grey eyes slid slowly over me, and he gave a slight nod to David. His presence had not escaped Jill either. As she settled herself at one of the tables, she remarked with satisfaction, 'I'm glad he's here. Now you'll be able to apologise.'

'Like hell I will!' I said explosively.

My sister ignored me. 'David, ask him to come and join us for a drink. There's no sign of Hazel and Dick yet, anyway.'

'How can I, he's with the Marshbanks girl. Anyway, it would be most embarrassing for Christy.'

'Damn Christy!' Jill said in a low voice. 'She's caused enough disturbance as it is. Your son's future is at stake!'

David stared at her in disbelief. 'Grow up, Jill, for God's sake!'

It was the first time I had heard him stand up to her, and the fact that it was on my behalf increased my discomfort. I glanced surreptitiously towards the bar, unwillingly conceding that off-duty the Headmaster admirably combined elegance with casualness. His dark grey trousers were narrow and well cut, his shirt a luminous shade of blue and the cravat tucked into the open neck a few shades darker. Morosely my eyes moved on to the girl at his side. She was laughing up at him over her glass, her long hair half screening her face, but I could see that she was tall, thin rather than slim, and dressed with the same nonchalant expensiveness as her companion. I looked quickly away, anxious not to be caught in my scrutiny, and lifted my glass to David. Out of the corner of my eye I saw that the girl was moving away to the dartboard, where a group of young people had gathered.

'Come and have a go, Nicholas!' she called. 'It doesn't matter if you win, we're used to it!'

He smiled and shook his head. Before I could stop her Jill leant forward.

'Mr Blair!'

I said violently, '*No*, Jill!' but he had turned, hesitated, and was coming over to the table.

Jill was saying charmingly, 'My sister was so upset by the embarrassment she caused you this afternoon. I do hope you'll forgive her.'

There was a brief pause, in which, presumably, he waited in vain for me to speak, then he said easily, 'There's nothing to forgive, Mrs Langley. I realise it will surprise Miss Drew, but there are no rules against freedom of speech for visitors! In fact, I found her views most—enlightening.'

I looked up at that to the full force of his gaze and knew that he was well aware that the apology was not of my making. He spoke directly to me.

'I gather you don't approve of our emphasis on discipline. I know the new idea is for complete self-expression, but without wishing to mount any soap-boxes, I personally am convinced that this can only lead to lack of security and a total disregard for other people.'

'I don't think,' I said acidly, stung to retort at last, 'that the permissive society would

36

totally engulf the school if a small amount of artistic licence were encouraged, but of course it's no concern of mine. No doubt you'll eventually turn out a nicely matching set of little grey-funnelled boys who never talk in corridors or carve their names on desks, but don't expect to find any geniuses among them!'

'Christy!' begged Jill desperately. There was a glint in Nicholas Blair's eyes.

'I'm afraid we must just agree to differ,' he said shortly. 'Good evening, Mrs Langley— Miss Drew.' He nodded to David, who had sat silent throughout the exchange, and went over to the dartboard to join his girl-friend.

'Oh, Christy, now look what you've done!' Jill was close to angry tears.

'It's your own fault for trying to make me apologise. I told you I wouldn't. Arrogant brute! He needs taking down a peg or two.'

I saw Nicholas Blair's companion glance over in our direction with a laugh, and wondered furiously what comment he had made. If she were the daughter of one of the governors she might already have heard of our meeting that afternoon. We had retreated then, we would not retreat now. To my intense relief a crowd of Jill and David's friends arrived and joined us and I forced myself to take part in the light conversation. Half an hour later Nicholas Blair and the girl left. I did not watch them go.

37

Even that was not to be my last encounter, for he was at church the following morning, accompanied by several masters and their wives—Tim's form-master among them—and three pews full of small boys. I was glad that at least we took our places in front of the school party, so that I could close my mind to them and concentrate on my surroundings.

The church was old and mellow and beautiful, and I was intrigued by the hour-glass fixed to the front of the pulpit. I hoped it wasn't still in use! Coats of arms of the local families hung along the walls and there was a huge wall painting of St Barnabas. David informed me in a whisper that this dated from the twelfth century, but the colours were as fresh as if it had been painted yesterday. Despite my misgivings of being reminded of the funeral there was no sadness here, just a great feeling of peace.

After the service I lingered behind a moment, mainly to look more closely at the painting, but also to give the party from Manor House time to get well clear of the church. When I eventually emerged into the sunshine I was relieved to find there was no sign of them, but Jill was standing talking and laughing in a group of people, and beckoned me across.

'Pamela has just invited us round for drinks on Tuesday,' she told me, after the introductions had been made.

'That's very kind, but I'd really meant to go

38

home on Tuesday,' I said tentatively.

'Oh, but you must stay for this!' the tall, pretty girl called Pamela insisted. 'We can't let you go home with the idea that we're just a bunch of rustics! You must meet some of the local celebrities—there are quite a few, you know, once you know how to dig them out!'

So I was committed to yet another day, I thought as we drove home. The two confrontations with Mr Blair had put a strain on the relationship between Jill and myself, nor did I find it easy to sit by and watch David's obvious unhappiness. On the other hand, though I was anxious now to end my stay with them, I was increasingly reluctant to leave Biddleton itself. I had a deep conviction that this was a place where I could find real happiness. Kimble's Cottage, never far from my thoughts, returned to haunt me, and before I could stop myself, I exclaimed, 'If only Kimble's Cottage could have been available!'

We were in the middle of Sunday lunch. I realised belatedly that David had been speaking, and everyone was staring at me in surprise.

'I'm sorry!' I said contritely. 'I was miles away.'

'Not very many miles, by the sound of it,' David remarked.

Jill laid down her knife and fork. 'But I thought you said you weren't interested in it?'

'How could I not be? It's absolutely perfect,

39

inside and out.'

'You've been inside? When?'

'The day I first saw it, with Mr Bannister.'

But when I mentioned it, you said it was too small!'

'I was just putting a brave face on it. I fell for it straight away, but since it was as good as sold I tried to put it out of my mind.'

Jill began to laugh. 'Oh, Christy, you're impossible! Why ever didn't you say so? I was convinced you weren't interested—you certainly gave that impression.'

'I don't see what's so funny.'

'Then I'll tell you—it's yours if you want it!'

I stared at her. *'Mine?'*

'You see, I knew old Mrs Kimble, I used to take her meals on wheels. When she became more or less completely bedridden, she told me she was going to live with her daughter in Bourton. I immediately asked her if I could have first refusal of the cottage. I thought it would be lovely to have you and Father so near, and out of that depressing place at home. I—hoped it would put new life into him. So I phoned Bill Selkirk and told him it was going up for sale and could I make a claim.'

I was only just half taking in what she said. 'Go on.'

'Well, Mrs Kimble didn't want people looking round while she was still there, so it only went on the market two weeks ago, when she left. By that time, of course, I knew that

Father was near the end, but it seemed even more suitable than ever for you.'

'But why didn't you tell me all this?'

'David said I should, but I didn't want to pressure you. I wanted you to make up your own mind.'

'And if I hadn't mentioned it again, you would have let it go without telling me?'

'I suppose so.'

I was aghast at the narrowness of my escape. Another thought struck me.

'What about the deposit?'

'Well, as soon as it was on the market, Bill was absolutely flooded with offers. I explained the position and asked him to hold it for me just for ten days, till you'd seen it.'

'But Mr Bannister said—'

'He probably didn't know anything about it. He was away at the time.'

I said a little shakily, 'It doesn't seem possible!'

'But it is!' Jill said excitedly. 'It will be lovely having you, Christy! Oh, I know you've had enough of me at the moment, but from now on you'll have your own front door to retreat behind!'

'After this,' I said fervently, 'I'll never complain about you again! Can we get hold of the keys and go there this afternoon?'

'I should think so.'

'Jill—seriously, I don't know what to say—'

'Then don't say anything.' She laid her hand

over mine. 'Perhaps it will make up a little for my being so selfish about not doing my share of looking after Father. It's been on my conscience, you know.'

David cleared his throat. 'Before you begin weeping in each other's arms, may I just say that for my part I'm delighted you're coming, Christy, and now do you think there's any chance at all of getting any pudding today?'

I spent the next two days going round and round my new home, planning what to bring from Bournemouth and what furniture would fit into the tiny cottage. I was not looking forward to selling the old house, but at least Biddleton would be waiting for me. I arranged to return home on the Wednesday morning so I could get things moving right away. But first, on Tuesday evening, was Pamela's cocktail party.

She and her husband lived at the end house of the same row as Jill's, so we hadn't far to go. Several of the people I had met on Saturday at the Falcon came up to chat to me, and I was quite enjoying myself when David said in my ear, 'Don't look now, but your friend's just arrived!' and across the throng of people I saw Nicholas Blair.

'I thought it was too good to be true!' I murmured. A moment later Michael Bannister touched my arm.

'I just had to tell you how glad I am about the cottage! You must think me a fool, but as I said, I've been away and knew nothing of the arrangement your sister had made with Bill.'

I smiled at him. 'I can hardly believe it's true!'

'Christy—' It was my hostess who caught hold of my elbow. 'Excuse me a moment, Michael, there's someone I'd like her to meet.' She propelled me across the room, threading her way through the groups of chattering guests, and to my consternation stopped in front of Nicholas Blair. 'Nicholas, I don't believe you've met Christy Drew, Jill Langley's sister.'

'As a matter of fact,' I broke in, 'we have met twice.'

'Oh? Well, do you know Robert and Val?'

'Pamela, can you come a minute?' a voice called from across the room.

'I'll leave the introductions to you then, Nicholas,' she said blithely, and left us, unaware of the embarrassment she had unwittingly caused.

Nicholas said gravely, 'Miss Drew, this is Robert Temple, my deputy head, and his wife, Valerie.'

I shook hands with them, liking them both at once, and turned back to Nicholas. 'I'm afraid I have some bad news for you, Mr Blair.'

'Oh?' A quizzical lift of one brow.

'I've just bought a cottage in the High Street. You won't be rid of me after all!'

43

His mouth twitched. 'But I'm delighted! Allow me to welcome you, on behalf of Biddleton!'

Robert Temple said, 'I may be obtuse, but why should you imagine that's bad news?'

Nicholas said smoothly, 'Miss Drew is a somewhat outspoken young lady, and on our previous meetings we haven't always seen eye to eye.'

'And she argued with you?' Robert Temple gave a laugh. 'Then I take my hat off to her!'

Nicholas said, 'You will appreciate that I only tolerate such insubordination because Robert is a very old friend, as well as being my deputy!'

Valerie laughed. 'Relax, Nicholas, you're off duty! And even if you insist on being so stuffy, I'm certainly not going to keep saying "Miss Drew". Hello, Christy, I'm Val! I'm delighted you're coming to live here, specially if you're able to keep Nicholas in his place!'

I said hastily, 'I make no claim to that!'

'I'm glad to hear it,' Nicholas observed drily. 'Miss Drew—'

' "Christy",' interrupted Val.

'—Christy,' continued Nicholas, after an infinitesimal pause, 'is not a person I'd like to cross swords with too often.'

'And that, from you, is a compliment!' said Robert Temple.

Jill called me and I excused myself to go and join her.

'You'll be relieved to know Nicholas Blair and I are not only on speaking terms but first name terms as well!' I told her with a bubble of laughter.

'Isn't that rather going from one extreme to the other? Still, I suppose it's an improvement! You know Michael, of course.'

He smiled at me. 'Could I cash in on the first-name basis too?'

'Be my guest!'

I liked Michael Bannister, there was something sincere and reliable about him— someone you could depend on, I thought. Jill moved away to join another group, and he said,

'I'm sorry to hear you're leaving tomorrow—I was hoping perhaps you'd have dinner with me.'

'I'd like to very much, but I want to get things underway at the other end now, so I can get back here as soon as possible.'

'Amen to that, anyway. Perhaps when you come back, then?'

'Yes, of course.'

'In the meantime, give me your glass and I'll find you a refill.'

Across the room, I saw that Nicholas and the Temples were preparing to leave. A moment later his voice, just behind me, said quietly, 'Christy—'

I turned.

'Sorry, that was rather forced on you, wasn't

it? Would you rather I reverted to "Miss Drew"?'

'Whichever you prefer,' I replied carefully, leaving the ball firmly in his court.

'Well, I just wanted to tell you that from now on the boys will be allowed more freedom in the studio.' His eyes mocked me. 'So you won the first round after all.'

I was completely taken aback and felt the colour flood my face.

'Oh, look, I'm not really trying to run your school for you!'

'No, but you happened to be right. It had never struck me before, but there was a kind of—mass-produced look about those paintings. I'm grateful to you for bringing it to my attention.'

Before I could think of anything else to say, he gave a curt little nod and was gone.

At my side David said, 'What was all that about?'

I answered numbly, 'The boys are to be given more freedom in their art.'

'My God!' David gazed at me with awe. 'You've only been here a week, but you've certainly set the village by its ears! Concessions from Nicholas Blair and invitations from Michael Bannister—two of the pillars of the community! There's obviously no holding you!'

I grinned at him. 'And I haven't really started yet!' I said happily.

CHAPTER FOUR

The next few weeks were not very happy for me. Even with the comforting knowledge of Kimble's Cottage and Biddleton behind me, it was not easy to put so definite an end to the whole of my previous life. There was the house to be put up for sale and the vast majority of the furniture auctioned. Jill had given me a list of the things she would like, and there were one or two I wanted for myself. Very little of the furniture, large and cumbersome as it was, would even fit into Kimble's Cottage. Mainly out of sentiment I decided to keep my own bedroom suite and a rocking chair. I would have liked the old kitchen table, whose white scrubbed top was so intricately bound up with childhood memories and whose surface had borne my first proud attempts at pastry and cake-making. But the minute kitchen at the cottage could only accommodate a drop-leaf table, and this it already had.

Father's solicitors were helpful, as were the estate agents they had put me in touch with, though I wished Michael Bannister could have been there instead. Then, at the last moment, I had an incredible stroke of luck. A syndicate approached me with the intention of turning the house into a private hotel, and they were prepared to buy the furniture too, lock, stock and barrel. It was a happy solution. I had feared that the house would be mutilated into flats, or, worse still, demolished completely for the land it stood on. It was a comfort to know that it would continue much the same as it had always been. Apparently Bournemouth still had room for one more private hotel.

Jill phoned me regularly, keeping me up to date on the progress of the contract for the cottage, and one day I received the registered packet for my signature. The last few days at Bournemouth dragged by, but at least I was spared the unhappiness of seeing the house dismantled and sold off piecemeal. Resolutely I stopped looking back, and concentrated all my efforts into looking forward.

The great day arrived at last. The removal men collected the things Jill and I had earmarked, I filled my little car with boxes of cutlery, crockery and linen, and we were away.

It had been arranged that I should go back to Jill and David's until the cottage was ready for occupation. I wanted to give it a quick coat of paint throughout and I should also have to find some more furniture. Yet even though I wasn't moving directly into my own house, as I turned the corner by the duckpond to drive up Biddleton High Street, I was aware of a singing sensation of coming home.

That first night David was out at a company dinner and Jill and I sat a long time over our meal, while the daylight faded outside. Neither of us made a move to switch on the lights. In the distance we could hear the soft strains of Ginette's transistor from her room. The boys were long since asleep. From the garden next door came the intermittent braying of a mowing machine.

Jill reached across and plugged in the coffee percolator again, and a moment later its bubbling gurgled gently like a contented goldfish.

'This is what I wanted,' she said, 'just the two of us, able to talk or not talk as the mood took us.'

'The two of us?' I repeated quizzically. 'What about David?'

'Yes,' she echoed flatly, 'what about David? What's the matter with me, Christy? I hate myself for it, but he irritates me so much I could scream!'

Despite my own observations when I had been with them, her words came as an unpleasant shock and I instinctively tried to make her retract them.

'Oh no, Jill, surely you're exaggerating!'

'I'm not, you know. He's good and kind and dependable—and he bores me to tears!'

I said sharply, 'Then you'd better start counting your blessings. A good husband, a lovely home, two healthy boys—'

'Do you think I haven't tried?' she broke in impatiently. 'Every night I seem to fall asleep to the same—the same litany: a good husband, a lovely home, etc. That might be enough if I were forty-seven, but I'm not, Christy! I'm twenty-seven, and I'm not ready to be bogged down with genteel country life and good works!'

'You should have thought of that before you got married,' I said tightly.

'Yes. You know what I often think? I should have left David to you. You could have made him happy.'

'Thank you very much.'

'Oh, don't be prickly, you know what I mean. You're calm and placid and reasonable, just like he is.'

'You make us sound as dull as ditch-water!'

She didn't deny it. 'I know I'm the one at fault, and it frightens me rather.'

'Frightens?'

She looked up, and her large eyes were almost purple in the half-light.

'With all the attractive men in the world, suppose I fell for one of them?'

'Just don't.'

'Suppose I couldn't help it?'

'There's always a point when you *can* help it, right at the beginning. You either let it happen or you put it completely away from you.'

'I think what I meant is that I might not *want* to stop myself. What then?'

"That would make it harder, but not impossible.'

'I'm not as strong-willed as you are,' she said plaintively, refilling our coffee cups. 'If a man attracts me, and I attract him—well, why the hell shouldn't I seize my chances? David is so *predictable*!' she added in a savage undertone. 'He even says exactly the same thing every time he makes love to me!'

I closed my eyes involuntarily against this betrayal. For a wild moment I longed for the loneliness of Bournemouth. At least I wasn't the unwilling recipient of such distressing confidences there.

'Please let me talk, Christy. You can see I never could to anyone else and I do so need to thrash it out with someone outside myself. I'm so *miserable*!'

'Does David know how you feel?'

'Vaguely. He just looks hurt when I snap, which makes it worse.'

'Can't you try talking it over with him?'

'What in heaven's name could I say? The fault's all on my side, I know that, but it doesn't help at all.'

We were silent for a long time. I had the impression that there was more she wanted to say but was hesitating, afraid of saying too much all at once. Perhaps she wanted me to become accustomed to one idea at a time. For my part, I had heard quite enough and made no attempt to help her. The lawnmower had apparently been put away for the night. A host of tiny flies veiled the window, but we had no

51

light to lure them inside.

At last she said dejectedly, 'There must be more to life than this.'

I roused myself, searching my mind for helpful suggestions. 'Have you thought of taking a job?'

'God, that's not what I meant!'

'It would give you an outside interest.'

'You've been reading the agony columns again! No, love, it's not a job I want, it's just— well, some excitement. It's ghastly to wake up every morning and know exactly what's going to happen during the day. Hardly worth getting out of bed!'

'There are a lot of people who'd be only too happy to swop with you.'

'Don't moralise, Christy. Are you one of them?'

The question startled me. A month ago, though I might not have admitted it, the answer would have been an unhesitating 'yes'. Now, with a new life opening up, a new circle of friends and an interesting contract awaiting my attention, I was not so sure. My own life seemed pretty good at the moment. It was true that she had David and I didn't. He had been a kind of trump card in my mind for so long that I was privately surprised at my hesitation now.

'Well, are you? Do you envy me?'

'I don't envy you exactly, no, but I think you're very lucky. You've got all the basic ingredients, it's up to you what you make of them.'

'The boys break up in another month,' she said irrelevantly.

'Yes, I suppose so.'

'David's people expect us to go down to their farm in Dorset again. It'll be deadly, but I suppose we'll have to go. What about you? Would you like to come?'

'I? Oh no, thanks. Just because I've moved into the same area you don't have to feel responsible for me, you know! I've only just got here, I've no wish to go away again. I'll be glad of the chance to settle down.'

'We can probably lend you the odd table and chair, if you're stuck, till you find something suitable.'

'Thanks. I haven't unpacked all my art things—they're still in the boot. I'll put them straight up in the studio as soon as I've given it a coat of paint.'

'David said he'd give you a hand at the weekend.'

'That would be a great help.' I stretched sleepily. 'Well, it's been a long day and I think I'm ready for bed.' I paused. 'Don't let things get you down, Jillie. They'll probably seem better in the morning.'

'I surely hope so. Thanks for listening, anyway. Goodnight, Christy—sleep well.'

'Goodnight.' I left her sitting in the almost-dark and went up to bed.

*　　　　*　　　　*

David was as good as his word, and by ten o'clock on Saturday morning we were up our respective ladders working feverishly. At about twelve Jill came round with sandwiches and a thermos of coffee. She perched herself on one of the rungs and watched us.

'I can't offer to help, because I've got to go and collect Timmy soon and I can hardly arrive at the school covered in paint!'

'You note the assumption that she'd be covered in it?' David remarked. 'Whatever Jill paints, she always manages to get it in her hair—don't ask me how!'

'I tilt my head to inspect the result and it kind of brushes against the wet surface. Anyway, I'm wearing a new dress—I can't take any chances.'

'It's a good excuse, I'll say that.'

She looked up at me wickedly. 'Mr Blair wouldn't approve if I turned up in dungarees, I'm sure!'

'So he's still ruling the roost, is he?' I reached up to the far corner of the ceiling, teetering precariously.

'Except in the art studios, yes!'

'I'm glad I was able to strike one blow for freedom!'

'Just don't strike any more—my nerves won't stand for it!'

We all jumped as the doorbell sounded

54

through the empty house. I'd forgotten the electricity had been reconnected.

'I'll go,' Jill offered, and ran down the stairs. Her voice reached us clearly. 'Oh, hello, Michael! Come on up!'

A moment later she reappeared with Michael Bannister behind her.

'Hello, Christy, welcome home! Wasting no time, I see!'

'No onlookers permitted,' David informed him, 'with the honourable exception of my wife. So take your jacket off and help yourself to a brush!'

'Press-ganged, no less!' Michael said with a laugh. 'Right—I came to offer my services, anyway.'

The three of us worked steadily throughout the weekend, and I continued by myself on Monday and Tuesday. By Wednesday, prepared to overlook the lack of carpets, I was ready to move in. David contacted the firm who had stored the Bournemouth furniture for the last few days, and on Thursday evening Jill, David, Michael and I gathered in the living room and toasted ourselves and each other in the champagne Michael had brought with him. I had taken up residence in Kimble's Cottage.

For the next two weeks I was less than sociable. I was working hard on a design, and all my spare time was taken up setting the cottage to rights. I borrowed Jill's sewing machine to run up the curtains, and found a couple of rugs in an arty shop in the next village. Slowly and surely it was beginning to take on the aspect of home.

One afternoon Jill phoned, full of apologies. 'Christy, could you possibly collect the boys for me today? David's suddenly sprung a dinner with some business friends, and the only time the hairdresser can take me is three-thirty. Ginette's bogged down with a pile of ironing, and if I take her away from it it'll never get done.'

'Yes, all right, I'll get them. Three-thirty for Mark and four for Tim?'

'That's right. Bless you, Christy.' She rang off and I went back to my desk. It was only later, as I strolled across the High Street to the village school, that I registered that I was still in shirt and trousers. Well, I was not going to change now. Jill could be the fashion plate if she wanted, I had other things to think about.

'Hello, Auntie Christy!' Mark yelled, flying towards me and catching hold of me round the knees as was his custom. 'Are we going back to your house?'

'No, we most certainly are not! I'll take you home when we've collected Tim—Mummy's at the hairdresser's. Let's walk round behind the church to pick up the car, then it'll be time to go.'

I held his hand as we crossed the road, though it obviously offended his dignity, and we walked round the church and Rectory to the lane which led off the main road to Jill's house and dropped down behind the village street.

'Can I open the garage door?' Mark asked, and without waiting for a reply, snatched the key-ring out of my hand and ran helter-skelter down the uneven surface of the lane. I followed anxiously, convinced he could not avoid falling, but he remained miraculously upright.

'Give me back the keys, please, I don't want to lose them.'

'I know this is for the garage and this is for the house, but what's that one for?'

'The garden door. It hasn't a handle and needs the key to open it.'

'Mummy said when she was a little girl she had a book about a secret garden behind a locked door.'

'Yes, but I'm afraid this one isn't very secret!'

We were bumping down the rough lane. It was strictly an access road, mainly used by the shops lower down the hill whose delivery vans were not allowed to park in the High Street. At the bottom we turned right and emerged by the Market Square.

'There's the Shipton Court Hotel,' Mark remarked a moment later. 'We had tea there once with Granny and Grandpa Langley. We're going to their farm in the holidays— they have horses and cows and all kinds of things!'

'That should be fun.' I slowed down and turned off the road through the gates of Manor House.

'Now, where will Tim be waiting?'

'He's usually at the top of the drive.' But not today. We sat in the car for a few minutes, but when Tim didn't appear I got out and called to a small boy who was passing, 'Do you know where Tim Langley is?'

'I think he's on the field practising.'

'Then it's time he wasn't,' I muttered. I looked down at Mark. 'Where is the field?'

'Round at the far side.'

'Are we allowed to go there?'

The front door of the school house behind us opened, and Nicholas Blair walked over to join us. He looked as immaculate as ever, and I was uncomfortably aware of the smudge of paint on my shirt.

'Well, well, if it isn't Crusading Christy! Welcome back to Manor House!'

'Thanks,' I said shortly.

'Hello, Mark.'

'Hello, sir.' Mark's eyes were firmly fixed on his scuffling shoe.

'Mark?' I repeated sarcastically. 'Surely it's not good for discipline to call them by their Christian names?'

'At the moment,' returned Nicholas blandly, 'he is still Mark. Naturally, when he comes to school he will be Langley Minor. I presume you're now awaiting Langley Major?' His eyes were amused at my discomfiture. I'd forgotten how damnably good-looking he was.

'I am. It's after four, I believe.'

'Yes, they're practising for Sports Day. They shouldn't be long now.' Behind us a queue of cars had drawn up and Nicholas moved away to explain the delay to politely patient parents. The charm could certainly be turned on when he felt like it, I thought sourly.

'Auntie Christy!' Tim came running in a crowd of other small boys, faces flushed and hair damp with exertion.

'I won my heats!' he cried. 'You are coming to Sports Day, aren't you?'

'I don't think so, Tim,' I said quietly, aware of Nicholas's strolling return.

'Oh, but you must! You want to see me win, don't you, and Daddy's in the Fathers' Match!'

'Of course you must come,' put in Nicholas smoothly, 'if only to satisfy yourself of fair play. I assure you there won't be a horsewhip in sight!'

'Don't destroy my illusions, please,' I said acidly, aware of the boys' faint bewilderment.

'Daddy's very good at cricket,' put in Mark tentatively.

'So's Mr Fenton,' said his brother gloomily. He looked up at Nicholas, greatly daring. 'Will you be playing, sir?'

'Very probably.'

'In the Fathers' Match?' I asked, bewildered

59

in my turn.

'Fathers v. Masters,' explained Tim with heavy masculine patience.

'Oh, I see.' Feeling foolish, I nodded to Nicholas and shepherded the boys back to the car.

'See you on Saturday!' he called after us.

Naturally the engine stalled. I was not in the best of tempers as I drove my nephews home, which seemed to be the effect that Nicholas Blair always had on me. And what was worse, it appeared that I'd committed myself to attending Sports Day too, which I could well have done without.

'Thanks for the lift!' they said dutifully, as they scrambled out of the car, and Tim added, 'I'll ask Mum and Dad to call for you on Saturday.'

CHAPTER FIVE

Uncharitably, I had hoped for rain, but Saturday dawned hot and sunny. Jill phoned in the morning.

'I hear you've been coerced into joining us this afternoon?'

'Afraid so, yes.'

'No need to sound so enthusiastic! Actually, I'll be glad to have someone to sit and talk to while David's making a fool of himself on the pitch! You'll be expected to yell encouragement, I warn you.'

'What time will you pick me up?'

'About a quarter to two, if you can be ready by then. They like to start prompt at two, otherwise it goes on too late. There'll be a refreshment tent, anyway, and I believe there's always strawberries and cream.'

'I can hardly wait!'

There was an air of intense excitement in the car, generated by Mark, who was bouncing up and down beside me on the back seat. He informed me that there was a Younger Brothers' Race for which he had entered—'though Mummy won't go in for the egg-and-spoon race. You will, won't you, Auntie Christy?'

'No, thank you, I'm with Mummy on this!' I did not intend to afford the supercilious Mr

Blair any more amusement at my expense. Crusading Christy, indeed! It still rankled.

The sports field at Manor House milled with men and small boys in white and women in brightly coloured dresses. Tim waved frantically to attract our attention to a row of chairs he'd been reserving for us, and we made our way over to him.

'Can I have a lemonade, Dad? The stand's just behind.'

'Not yet, for heaven's sake! You'll be so full of gas you won't be able to run!'

With an excruciating burst of sound, the loudspeakers started blaring a military tune. It all reminded me of the gymkhanas of my youth.

'Hello, Mrs Langley. Are you completely deafened?'

I turned back to find Jill smiling up at the tanned, attractive face of Mr Fenton, Tim's form-master.

'Hello, Miss Drew—nice to see you again.' In sports flannels he looked younger than ever. His brown-gold hair grew down into modest sideburns glinting in the sunshine. He made me think of a healthy young animal eager for the contest. He gestured comically towards the loudspeaker, which was more than a match for anyone, shrugged his shoulders resignedly and moved away. We sat down and I felt in my bag for my sunglasses. Jill, I noticed, had come in a sleeveless, low-necked dress, determined to lose no opportunity of sunbathing. Her skin was already a rich golden brown and showed to great advantage against the pale lilac of her dress and, I thought wryly, against my own pale arms.

The races began, fifty metres for the younger ones, progressing to seventy for the 'senior boys' of eleven and twelve. The sun beat down mercilessly and I feared that my look of enthusiasm was beginning to become rather fixed. There was an awful sameness about those races, when Tim's was the only face I knew. We moved inexorably through obstacle, slow bicycle and three-legged. More and more people were drifting to the lemonade stand behind our chairs, but I longed above all for a cup of tea.

'Not till four o'clock, I'm afraid,' Jill said sympathetically in answer to my anguished query. 'It'll all be over then, except for the Grand Finale of the Fathers' Match. We'll make a discreet withdrawal so as to get to the tea tent ahead of the crowd.'

Tim excelled himself by winning the fifty metres and the three-legged race for his house, and Mark did creditably by coming second in the Younger Brothers' Race.

'All we need is a century from David and we can retire covered in glory!' I said facetiously.

'You may mock,' David answered darkly, 'but you might have to eat your words. I'm a wizard with a cricket bat!'

'A pity your accomplishments are so limited, darling!' said Jill lightly. He smiled, but not before I had seen the hurt in his eyes. My palm itched to slap my sister's beautiful face.

Mr Fenton was standing just inside the tea tent with his wife, to whom he introduced us. She looked pale and her forehead was beaded with perspiration.

'I'm afraid the heat's too much for her,' Mr Fenton said. 'Come and sit over here and rest for a bit, dear.'

'I'm sorry, Barry, I think I'll have to go home.'

'Oh, not before the match, surely!'

'I don't think I could face it.'

'We need all the support we can muster, you know, with all the little brats yelling for their fathers!'

'It must be rather like an "away" match,' I said smilingly.

'It certainly is. Believe me, the cheers when one of us is caught out are galling, to say the least.'

'Barry—please—'

'All right, I suppose if you must, you must.'

'Have you far to go?' I asked.

'No, we've one of the cottages in the grounds—only two minutes away.'

'You won't get much peace, then, with the loudspeaker making such a row,' remarked Jill.

'It'll be all right if I can just lie down and

close my eyes. I'm sorry to be such a wet blanket.'

Her husband took her arm and led her out of the tent.

'Pretty obvious what her trouble is,' I murmured.

'What?' Jill turned and looked at me. 'Oh—do you think so?'

'I should say it was highly likely. Poor girl—he doesn't strike me as the most considerate of husbands.'

'Why not?'

'He's letting her go with a pretty poor grace. I've a feeling that if we hadn't been here, he'd have tried to talk her into staying, in which case she'd probably have passed out on him.'

Jill drained her cup and put it on the trestle table. 'If you're ready I suppose we'd better be getting back, or we'll lose our places.'

'I don't think I could face all that sun again—I sympathise with Mrs Fenton. You go, if you want to continue the tanning process.'

'Are you sure you don't mind? We'll see you at the car afterwards, then.'

I watched her walk out into the glare again and stop to talk to a group of parents. Laughingly they all moved on together. I left the tent and made my way over to the opposite side of the field by the pavilion, which was now in the shade. I could see Jill and the boys in our old seats. David came down the pavilion steps and joined me.

'Hello, is the sun too much for you?'

'Yes. Are you batting first?'

'Our side is. I'm fourth man. I'm told the headmaster bowls a wicked ball.'

'I can imagine.'

The masters came out of the pavilion and took up their places on the field. Nicholas, I saw, was going to bowl the first over. We watched as he ran and hurled the ball, and a second later the stumps were spreadeagled behind the batsman.

'A great start!' said David gloomily.

There were boos and groans and a sympathetic spatter of applause for the shame-faced father who walked off the field two minutes after walking on. The next man went in to loud cheers, and was very nearly caught by the wicket-keeper. After that they settled down, treating Nicholas's bowling with much more respect. Twenty minutes later, David left me to buckle on his pads and I sat down by myself. Cricket, I had to admit, did not set my pulses racing. However, I clapped hard for David, and he made a very useful fifty before being stumped by one of Nicholas's most devilish spins. With an eye on the clock, the Fathers declared at two hundred for seven. Nicholas and Barry Fenton were the opening batsmen for the Masters.

I watched with exasperation the smooth swipes with which Nicholas despatched ball after ball into boundary. Was there nothing this infuriating man couldn't do? The boys, as strictly partisan a crowd as it had been my misfortune to encounter, greeted each superb stroke with boos and jeers, but they went wild with delight when Barry Fenton was caught for thirty-seven. Nicholas had made over seventy, and the chances for the Fathers were looking extremely thin when his partner forced him into an unwise extra run and he was run out. The boys roared with glee. There was no recognition at all of the magnificent performance the headmaster had put in, except from one fair-minded parent, who applauded as he reached the edge of the field.

I had never in my wildest dreams expected to feel sorry for Nicholas Blair, but I did now. He had played superbly, both as bowler and batsman, in face of what amounted almost to crowd-hostility. That his own side would applaud him later I had no doubt, but I felt it was up to me, on behalf of the spectators, to offer a word of congratulation. There was weariness in every line of his body as he came towards me. He hadn't seen me, but as he approached I said spontaneously, 'Well played!'

He stopped, leaning on his bat. 'Well, thanks! I certainly didn't expect that! Come and join me in a glass of lemonade.'

He leant his bat nonchalantly against the pavilion steps and took my arm, leading me through the throng to the stall on this side of the field. Our progress was hampered by people coming up to congratulate him. Obviously my own contribution hadn't been as necessary as I'd supposed, but I didn't regret offering it.

He raised his glass to me and commented, 'So you came after all.'

'As you see.'

'Have you enjoyed it?'

'Well, to coin a phrase, when you've seen one race, you've seen them all!'

Nicholas laughed. 'My own sentiments exactly, but not a word to anyone! How are you settling down in Biddleton?'

'Oh, very well. I've been pretty busy these last few weeks, so I haven't been able to explore the surrounding countryside yet.'

'What exactly does graphic designing entail?'

'A multitude of things. At the moment I'm designing a new package for a baby food. Last month it was garden furniture. It's the variety that appeals to me, really.'

'And you're freelance, presumably, since you were able to come here?'

'Yes. After my mother died six years ago I worked from home to keep Father company. It fitted in very well.'

'And now?'

'He died in May.'

'I see. I'm sorry. So your sister suggested you should come here?'

'She brought me back for a holiday, but I fell for both the village and the cottage at once.'

An outburst of applause pulled our attention back to the match.

'That appears to be the end,' Nicholas remarked. 'I'm afraid I must go, I'm needed to present prizes.' He turned back. 'And Christy—thanks for the moral support, I needed it.'

He was gone before I could think of a reply, leaving me in the grip of conflicting emotions. I had still not sorted them out when I let myself into the cottage to hear the telephone ringing. I caught it up and said breathlessly, 'Hello?'

'Hello indeed!' It was Michael Bannister's voice. 'I was just about to give up. Where on earth were you? I've been ringing all afternoon.'

'Cheering on my nephews at Manor House sports.'

'Good God, how did you get roped in for that?'

'I've no idea,' I said truthfully.

'Are you on your knees?'

'Just about.'

'Think you could find sufficient energy to come out and have a meal with me?'

'Oh, Michael, I'd love to!' Nice, uncomplicated Michael!

'Marvellous. I'll pick you up about eight.'

"I'll be ready.'

I looked ruefully at my hot, sticky reflection in the mirror and then at my watch. Half-past six. Just time for a leisurely bath and hair-wash.

He arrived as the clock struck eight and held both my hands while he surveyed me approvingly. 'Lovely! Cool and crisp and just right!'

'Thank you, sir!' I picked up my handbag and pulled the door shut behind us. 'I could just do with a nice, relaxing meal after the strains of the afternoon.'

'I don't doubt it. You didn't actually compete, did you?'

'Not on your life!'

He laughed and opened the car door. 'Well, we won't go far afield this time. They do a very good meal at the Shipton Court. I booked a table for eight-thirty—it's popular on Saturday nights—so we've time for a couple of drinks first.'

We were there in under five minutes, and judging by the number of cars in the car-park Michael had been wise to book a table. The cocktail bar was crowded and I recognised several people I had met at Pamela's.

'Now,' Michael said, settling down next to me on the bench seat, 'tell me all about yourself!'

'That won't take long. You know it already. But I don't know anything about you.'

70

'No, you don't, come to think of it. Thanks for taking me on trust!'

'Have you a dark and dangerous past, then?' I asked flippantly.

'Neither dark nor dangerous, but a past of sorts, certainly. Did you know, for instance, that I've been married?'

I turned to face him. 'No, I didn't.'

'My wife died four years ago. I have a daughter of seventeen.'

'Seventeen! But you don't look old enough!'

He laughed. 'For which, thanks!'

'I'm sorry about your wife. It must have been hard, with a young girl, too.'

'Yes, it was hard. It took quite a lot of getting over.'

'You didn't have to tell me, you know.'

'I wanted to. In any case, as you've been seen with me tonight, someone would be sure "just to mention it" to you by tomorrow morning at the latest!'

'Where's your daughter now?'

'At her last term of boarding school. In October she starts at university.'

'So you won't even have her company when she leaves school?'

He shrugged. 'She has her own life to lead.'

'But you must get lonely.'

'Yes, I do.' The simple statement spoke volumes.

I said again, 'I am sorry, Michael.'

He smiled and patted my hand. 'Don't look

so sad, I'm well acclimatised now. And at least I can have an evening out with a pretty girl now and then! But what about you—don't you get lonely sometimes?'

'Not really. My father was a very stimulating companion, and I would have been lost without him, but Jill, bless her, dreamed up this idea of my coming here, and it's been marvellous. One thing that so appealed to me about Kimble's Cottage that first day was its position right in the centre of the village. I knew there'd be plenty going on around me all the time.'

A waiter materialised beside us. 'Your table's ready, Mr Bannister.'

We went through into the large, square dining-room. The late evening sunlight streamed through the window on to a huge bank of beautifully arranged flowers. There was a low buzz of conversation and a string quartet played discreetly on a raised platform at the far end of the room. I felt pleasantly tired and content. I settled in my chair and my eyes went idly round the diners and skidded to a startled halt as they encountered the steady gaze of Nicholas Blair. He must have watched us come in. His companion was the girl who had been with him at the Falcon. As our eyes met I half smiled and he inclined his head formally. I turned hurriedly back to Michael, somewhat disconcerted to discover he had witnessed the exchange. In a sudden lull I heard Nicholas's companion say clearly,

'Who *is* that girl?'

Michael said softly, 'Don't let him rile you. He makes a habit of it.'

'You don't like him, do you?'

'I didn't say so.'

'When he was mentioned before, you called him one of the main tourist attractions.'

'You've had a chance now to discover what I meant.'

'But what have you actually got against him?'

'Oh, I don't know. He's just so damned suave and sure of himself, that's all. We've had the odd brush from time to time. Clash of personalities, I suppose you'd call it.'

I said in my turn, 'Who's that girl he's with?'

'Lydia Marshbanks. God knows what he sees in her, other than the fact that she's her father's daughter. Loaded, of course. Perhaps that's the attraction.'

'My, my! You have got it in for him!' I said lightly. 'Poor Nicholas! I hope you don't meet him on a dark night!'

'Ah yes, I'd forgotten you were on first-name terms. Perhaps I've been speaking out of turn.'

'Not really.' I was more nettled than I would admit by the curt nod which had been his only acknowledgment of me, after the easy friendliness of this afternoon. 'Anyway, don't let's waste the whole evening talking about

Nicholas Blair.'

'I'm with you there. Now, tell me about the work you're doing. I know very little about it, but it sounds fascinating.'

We steered clear of Nicholas after that. Occasionally, by mistake, my eyes drifted in his direction, but he seemed deeply engrossed in his companion. Several times her clear laugh rang out. Ridiculously, beneath the cover of my chatter with Michael, I found myself regretting that I had gone to his support that afternoon. How stupid to imagine that he could ever be in need of anyone. They left before we did, without a glance in our direction.

Quite suddenly, I was extremely tired. The heat and strain of the afternoon took their toll at one and the same time. I could hardly keep my eyes open.

'Michael, I'm very tired. Would you mind if we went home?'

'Of course not.'

I watched him as he beckoned to the waiter and paid the bill. Sherry-coloured hair, sherry-coloured eyes, a firm but gentle mouth. An attractive man, certainly. My thoughts went automatically to David, as they always did for comparison with anyone, and I realised with faint surprise that they were a lot alike.

'A penny for them!'

'As a matter of fact, I was just thinking you're rather like David.'

'Oh? In what way?'

'I don't know. It's hard to pinpoint. Perhaps it's that you're both—vulnerable.' The word was out before I'd had time to weigh its implications.

Michael said slowly, 'That's a somewhat astute observation. I don't know about David, but you're probably right on my account.'

'It was only a passing thought,' I said hurriedly—but it was rather a disconcerting one, all the same.

CHAPTER SIX

For the next week or two I was working very hard on a series of designs. I didn't see much of Jill, and I turned down a couple of invitations from Michael, pleading pressure of work. Even after such concentrated effort, the deadline for the designs was perilously close, and rather than entrust them to the vagaries of the post, I decided to deliver them personally to my clients. Accordingly I drove to Moreton-in-Marsh to catch the London train. It was a good one, just under two hours, which was the same as it had been from Bournemouth.

London in mid-July was hot and airless, and I thought longingly of my cool little terrace at home. But the journey was well worth while. The clients were delighted with my efforts and insisted on taking me out for dinner before I caught the train home.

It was therefore well after eleven by the time I had collected my car at Moreton and driven to Biddleton. I put it away and walked through the shadowed garden round to the front door. Suddenly my heart was in my mouth. A car was parked at the gate. For a moment I was distinctly nervous. Then I told myself that this was Biddleton, and I could come to no harm if I went to see who it was. As a precaution I opened the front door and switched on the light before starting down the path, and by that time the man in the car had got out and was walking up to meet me. It was David. The relief that swamped me was short-lived. His face as he came into the light was haggard.

'David, what's happened? What on earth are you doing here at this time of night?'

'I must talk to you, Christy.'

'Of course. Come in. Where's Jill?'

'At home. Now.'

I stood aside to let him pass and pushed the door shut. 'Go into the sitting room. I'll make some coffee. You look as though you could do with some.'

He moved past me like a sleepwalker. I ran to the kitchen, the horrible sense of impending crisis hanging over me. In less than two minutes I had put two steaming cups of coffee on a tray and carried them through. David was slumped forward in a chair, his head in his hands. I put the tray down in silence and drew both sets of curtains across the windows, shutting out the darkness.

As I came back to the table, he reached up blindly and caught hold of my hand. 'Christy, I'm nearly out of my mind!'

I stood staring down at his bent head, my mouth dry. 'What is it? What's happened?'

'It's Jill. She's having an affair.'

'Oh no! David, no! You must be mistaken! I know you're going through rather a sticky patch, she told me herself. And I know she's impatient and awkward sometimes, but it'll pass, I'm sure it will.'

He raised his head and stared at me. 'I saw her, Christy! I saw her, for God's sake!' His voice cracked.

'Where? Who with?'

'The master from that bloody school.'

Without warning, a picture of Nicholas flooded my mind, and with it came a shaft of pain which was totally unexpected.

I said sickly, 'It *can't*—'

'Barry Fenton.'

I stared at him, struggling to regain control, my breathing still ragged from shock.

'I recognised his car parked in a side lane along the Cheltenham road. I didn't think much of it, God help me, except "Rotten bastard—can't he wait till his wife's better?" It wasn't till I got home and Jill wasn't there— Even then it didn't really dawn until she did come, her eyes bright and her face glowing, in a vivid yellow dress. And all at once it hit me— that was the colour I'd seen in the back of the car. I was so shattered I asked her outright.'

I could feel him shaking, but I was powerless to help.

'What did she say?'

'Told me to mind my own business. Said she didn't ask where I was every time I went out.'

'So she didn't—admit it?'

'She didn't need to. It was all there in her

face. God, I love her!' He gave a harsh laugh. 'I haven't much pride, have I? Christy, what in heaven's name do I do now?'

'It—it may not be as bad as you think.'

'With Barry Fenton? I wouldn't give much for any woman's chances in the back seat of a car with him.'

I thought of the hot, assessing eyes, the sensual mouth, and could offer no comfort. There was a kind of animal magnetism about Barry Fenton that I hadn't encountered before; I didn't underrate its effectiveness. Jill had said: 'If a man attracts me and I attract him—' I remembered thinking there was more she had wanted to say. She'd probably had Barry in mind, even then.

David's eyes were still desperately on my face. I bent forward and kissed him gently. 'Hang on, love, the world hasn't come to an end. She's just lost her head for a while—she'll get over it. Drink your coffee while it's hot.'

I put the cup and saucer into his hand and sat back on my heels, trying to sift over what he'd said.

'Can I stay here tonight?' he asked after a moment. 'I'd be quite comfortable on the sofa.'

I shook my head slowly. 'No, David. You must stay with Jill tonight of all nights. Don't let her be able to say you were out all night.'

'You're right, of course,' he said dully. I saw him wince as he swallowed the scalding liquid, welcoming the pain of it.

'Could you speak to her?'

'I'll try, if you like.'

'I'd be very grateful.'

'There's one good thing about it—it's nearly the end of term. You're off to Dorset soon, aren't you? Stay there as long as you can, but take her about a lot—don't let her get bored. And don't let her trample all over you, either. Stand up to her a bit.'

He smiled crookedly. 'I told you I wasn't the masterful type.'

'Then work on it!'

He put down the cup and saucer and stood up and I stood with him. Gently he put his arms round me and held me against him. 'Bless you, Christy, you've done me a power of good. I knew you would.'

'I'll have a word with Jill tomorrow. Try to keep things on an even keel if you possibly can.'

'I'll try.'

I closed the door behind him and drew a long, tremulous breath. It had been a most revealing half hour, and not only because of Jill's transgressions. David had held me in his arms and I had felt—nothing. Nothing, that is, but genuine affection and sympathy for my sister's husband. After nine years the last of my old feelings for him had vanished without my even noticing it.

Something else occurred to me. David had

not jilted me, as I'd thought self-pityingly all these years, because he had never loved me in the first place. It was as simple as that. Loving him, I had read into his kisses more than had been there. To him I'd been just a casual girl-friend, and no doubt he imagined I'd felt the same way. Thank heaven he had never discovered otherwise.

I went slowly through to the bedroom, switching off lights as I went. Father had said David would never have been right for me. Perhaps initially it had been my strength that had appealed to his weakness, until his emotions were genuinely involved with Jill. And perhaps the same thing was happening again with Michael Bannister. They were both—vulnerable. Father was right. I would never have been happy with a man who was weaker than myself.

I washed and undressed, turning over these novel ideas in my mind. Then I switched off the light and climbed into bed. About Nicholas Blair I very carefully did not think at all.

I awoke the next morning with a sense of foreboding, which resolved itself as I became fully conscious into the realisation that I had pledged myself to speak to Jill. Since I didn't believe in postponing unpleasant duties, I drove round to her house at nine-thirty, when I judged she would have returned home from taking the boys to school.

She opened the door to me with an amused

smile. 'Come in, Christy, I was expecting you.'

She led the way into the sitting room, sat down demurely on the sofa and folded her hands. 'Right—fire away!'

'You're not making this very easy.'

'Why should I? I presume you've come at David's instigation to read the Riot Act?'

I said evenly, 'Have you any idea what you're doing to him?'

Her eyes flickered. 'It was unfortunate that he should find out, I admit.'

'Jill, you're not really—I mean—'

She gave a brittle laugh. 'No, love, not really. Not so far. Any more details I can supply?'

'Look,' I said furiously, 'you can sleep around the whole village for all I care, but I warn you—if any hurt comes to David or the boys I'll have nothing more to do with you— ever!'

That shook her. 'Christy, can we start again? Attack seemed the best method of defence, but I desperately want you on my side. I told you that before.'

'Do there have to be sides?'

'It would seem so. You can see the difference, can't you, between Barry and David?'

'Yes,' I said shortly, 'and I infinitely prefer David.'

She flushed and I thought helplessly for the hundredth time how lovely she was, with her mouth full and sulky, her eyes mutinously bright. If she had set her cap at Barry Fenton—and I rather feared it was that way round—he had no chance of resisting her.

I tried another tack. 'What about his wife, Jill?'

'What about her? If she can't hold him, she doesn't deserve him.'

'She's carrying his child!' I said brutally, and saw her wince. 'It's not love, you know, it's pure infatuation. For pity's sake let him go.'

Her mouth trembled. 'I can't, Christy. Really I can't.'

'It's nearly the end of term. Promise me you'll make no attempt to contact him during the holidays. With luck it'll all die a natural death with no real harm done.'

She shook her head helplessly. 'I can't—don't ask me.'

'Somebody has to—you wouldn't listen to David. You should have seen him last night, Jill, he was pathetic—'

'David's *always* pathetic, that's half the trouble.' She shot me a swift glance from under lowered lids. 'All right, I shouldn't have said that, and I *am* sorry he found out.'

'Meaning it would have been all right if he hadn't?'

'Christy, don't lecture me, please. I'm so mixed up, I don't know where I am.'

I leant forward and caught hold of her hands. 'Then promise me, promise, Jill, that

83

you won't contact him at all for the next month or two. I'll collect Tim next week, and then you'll be away. *Please*—surely your marriage is worth trying to save? I know David will do everything he can to meet you halfway.'

At last her eyes fell. 'All right, I promise.'

I drew a breath of relief. 'Good girl! Let your car go in for service or something, and I'll take over the school run. But tell Tim not to keep me waiting—I don't want to fall foul of Mr High and Mighty Blair!'

She smiled in spite of herself. 'All right. And—thanks, Christy.'

Somehow the next ten days crawled by. I took Jill out in the car a couple of times, had her and David round for supper. A precarious peace seemed to be prevailing. Nor, at the school, was there any sign of Nicholas. Perhaps it would all work out for the best. The boys broke up, the iron gates were closed, and David and his family went to Dorset for their holidays.

*   *   *

During the first fortnight in August I lived a deliciously lazy life. I had decided that although I wasn't going away this year, there was no reason why I shouldn't have a holiday. I lay out all day in my little back garden, and if my skin didn't go the gorgeous colour Jill's did, at least I acquired the pale honey-tan which was the most I could hope for.

One evening I went to a concert with Michael, and in the car coming home he kissed me. After a while he sat back and looked at me ruefully.

'Do you keep everyone at arm's length, or is it only me?'

'If that was arm's length, you're a pretty good long-distance operator!'

'You know what I mean. I'm not even at first base with you, am I?'

'Oh, come on, Michael, why so serious? It was a lovely evening and a lovely kiss. Isn't that enough?'

'No, I'm rather afraid it isn't.'

I said gently, 'Please let it be.'

He felt in his pocket for cigarettes. After a moment he said, 'Will you come home one evening and meet Liz? She went off with her pals for a working holiday in Spain, but she'll be back at the end of this week.'

'I'd like to—thanks.'

He said abruptly, 'Christy, is there any hope at all?'

'I don't know, Michael, really I don't. We haven't known each other very long, after all.'

'What has time got to do with it? I'm too old for you, of course, I realise that.'

'No, it's not that.'

'Then what is it?'

'Oh, Michael,' I said despairingly, 'please don't be so—so—'

'Vulnerable?'

'Yes.'

'You tried to warn me before, didn't you? Oh, forget it, I'm sorry to have embarrassed you. I knew how the land lay really, it was stupid of me to bring it up at all, but I just thought that as we're both alone— Never mind, love, it's just one of those things. Come and meet Liz, anyway. How about Thursday?'

So I did, and she was charming. Long straight hair, a ragged fringe on her forehead, 'Granny' clothes, but charming underneath it all. She cooked a simple but delicious supper and we all laughed a lot. Afterwards, as I helped her with the dishes, she said suddenly,

'Daddy's in love with you, isn't he?'

'I'm afraid he might be.'

'But you don't love him?'

'I don't know, Liz. I'm sorry.'

She said frankly, 'Don't be put off on my account, will you? I wouldn't be around much anyway.' Her clear grey eyes were fixed on my face. 'You'd be very good for him, I see that. I'm just not so sure that he'd be good for you.'

I gave a defensive little laugh. 'I see you believe in plain speaking.'

'You get things straightened out more easily that way.'

'No doubt. Would you like him to get married again?'

'Of course. Men are pretty useless on their own, aren't they?'

'It wouldn't worry you?'

'Usurping Mum's place, you mean? No,' she shook her head emphatically. 'I know how much he loved her—he just went to pieces when she died—but he needs someone else now. I'd like it to be you, but only if you're sure.'

'I wish I could be.'

The little conversation, inconsequential and unresolved, was going round in my head the next day as I gathered together paints and pad for my long-postponed attempt to capture some of the local scenery. I put a couple of hard-boiled eggs, some apples, cheese and a bottle of milk in a basket, and set off in the car, jolting down the lane and out on to the road past Shipton Court and Manor House. I had remembered seeing a particularly pretty spot along here, not far off the road—fields and a rising hill clothed with young trees. It was picturesque and would not require too much effort—a perfect holiday task.

I parked the car on the grass verge, collected all my goods and chattels and set off. After about a hundred yards, the field dipped into a hollow, screening me from the road. I set up my canvas chair, spread everything around me, and stood the milk bottle in the shade. It was very quiet apart from a lark several miles above me and the occasional whoosh of a passing car.

My mind was still full of Michael. Suppose I

did marry him without really loving him—could I make a go of it? Or would we finish up like Jill and David? Perhaps Jill and I were more alike than we'd realised. I, too, would lose patience with a man who always gave way to me, as, I knew instinctively, would Michael.

I worked steadily, my brush going briskly across the paper, and it was several moments before I registered that there was a shadow between me and the sun. I turned quickly, to find Nicholas Blair on the rise behind me.

'What on earth are you doing here?' I demanded ungraciously, to hide the fright he had given me.

'Your usual charming self, I see!'

'I thought you'd be miles away, lying on some Continental beach.'

'I'm afraid not. May I join you for a moment, or will it drive the muse away?'

'If you want to.'

He was wearing a white shirt and a pearl grey tie, and his jacket was slung over one shoulder. Strange, how his clothes always registered with me.

'Did you know I was here, or was it just the fickle finger of Fate?' I asked carelessly, returning to my work.

'As a matter of fact, I recognised your car. I'd seen it once or twice scuttling out of the gates during the last days of term.'

I ignored the implication. 'So you actually sought me out. I'm honoured. Why?'

'I felt like sharpening my wits on someone, and I thought "Who better than Christy?"'

'There was no need to come creeping up like that, frightening the life out of me.'

'I'm sorry, but there was a possibility you might have had the estate agent in tow. I didn't want to embarrass you!' He met my furious gaze blandly.

'Are you always so offensive, or do I just bring out the worst in you?'

'A bit of both, probably.'

He had come down the slope and, after a cursory glance at my work, settled himself on the grass.

'Will it disturb you if I talk?'

'It usually does!'

He looked up at me, eyes narrowed against the sun. 'We are vitriolic today, aren't we?'

I met his look for a moment, then I laughed. 'Okay. Sorry.'

'After all, I thought we'd made a little progress on Sports Day.'

'So did I, till I was withered by a glance at the Shipton Court.'

'Ah yes, I'm sorry about that. I was— somewhat taken aback to see you there.'

'I can't think why.'

'Nor can I, really. Except that I hadn't realised you were so thick with Michael Bannister.'

'No thicker,' I said sweetly, 'than you are with Lydia Marshbanks!'

He stared at me for a moment, then he gave a shout of laughter. 'Oh, Christy, you're quite a girl, aren't you?'

I kept my eyes firmly on my painting. After a moment I said, 'I gather you don't approve of Michael? If it's any comfort, it's entirely mutual.'

'You must have had a pleasant evening, listing my shortcomings.'

'Fascinating.'

'Am I allowed to know your conclusions?'

I turned to look at him, tapping the end of the brush against my teeth.

'It really boils down to the fact that you live in too rarefied an atmosphere.'

'Oh?'

'I mean, most business executives and so on leave all the "Yes sir, no sir" at the office at the end of the day, but you never get away from it, do you?'

'With the result that I have a somewhat inflated idea of my own importance!'

'I tried to avoid saying that!'

He pulled a blade of grass and chewed it thoughtfully. 'Interesting. You could be right. I'd no idea I was such a stuffed shirt.'

'I didn't say that, either. But I do think you should relax more.'

'So Val keeps telling me.'

'You can relax now, anyway,' I said kindly. 'The "God's Gift to Parents" angle doesn't carry any weight with me.'

'So I've noticed.' He leant back on one elbow. 'Well, that's your diagnosis—what cure would you prescribe?'

'Cure?'

'To counteract the deadly effects of the Rarefied Atmosphere!'

'I don't know, really. Possibly a course of re- as opposed to dehumanisation.'

'My God, is it that bad?'

I laughed. 'Not really, I suppose. But I don't know why you're asking me—I hardly know you, after all. If Lydia's satisfied, who am I to complain?'

'The world doesn't consist entirely of Lydia.'

'I got the impression that it did. Your world, that is. And the school, of course, but then they go rather well together, don't they?'

'And *that* was a little below the belt.'

'It wasn't meant to be.'

I concentrated on blending the exact shade I wanted for the yellowing grass and after a moment he lay back, his arms behind his head, staring up at the fathomless sky. There was silence except for the swishing of my brush and the plopping of the paint on the palette. I worked steadily, and when at last I glanced at my watch it was twelve-thirty.

'Lunch time!' I announced. I delved into the bag and tossed him an egg.

'No, really, I can't eat your lunch.'

'Try! But I warn you, it's not easy to be dignified eating an egg with your fingers!'

91

'So the treatment has begun!'

'There's cheese and apples and milk— somewhat frugal, I'm afraid, but you're welcome to half.'

'On one condition, then.'

'Being?'

'That you let me give you dinner.'

I looked at him in surprise. 'Isn't that rather drastic?'

'Very. Shows how hungry I am!'

We looked at each other and laughed together, for the first time. He said nonchalantly, 'You won't have to ask permission or anything, will you?'

'No, will you?'

'Positively not.'

'That's all right, then.' I threw him an apple and a triangle of cheese. 'A habit I learned from my Yorkshire grandmother.'

'I didn't know you had a Yorkshire grandmother.'

'Actually, I haven't.'

'That explains it. You know, it's an awfully long time since I talked nonsense like this. I must admit it's very refreshing.' He bit into his apple. 'Specially when it's intelligent nonsense!'

I laughed. 'That's the nicest thing anyone ever said to me!'

'In fact, I believe you're doing me good already.'

'I'm getting somewhat tired of being told I

do people good.' First David, then Liz on Michael's behalf, now Nicholas. 'I think I'll put myself inside a bottle labelled "To be taken three times a day after meals."'

'That sounds very Lewis Carroll.'

'It does, doesn't it? I'm afraid I've only got one straw.'

'What? Oh, the milk. Never mind, I'll drink from the bottle.'

'Progress indeed!'

I watched as he tilted back the bottle and drank, his black hair gold-tipped in the sun.

'That was lovely. What now? Are you going to paint again, or do you feel like a walk?'

'I think I've done enough for the moment. A walk would be fine.'

'Your things will be quite safe here. We'll collect them on the way back. If we go up that little hill and through the wood, there's a magnificent view the other side.'

He helped me to stack the things, draped his jacket over them, and we set off. I don't remember all the things we talked about that afternoon—it was just whatever came into our heads. Three-quarters of it was nonsense, anyway. Yet I had the feeling that underneath it all we were weighing each other up, carefully testing our reactions to each other.

The wood was dappled with sunshine, smelling dustily of bark and dry mosses, and our footsteps sounded loud in the silence. As we emerged on the far side the valley lay spread before us. We sat on a large rock, and there wasn't another person in sight as far as the eye could see.

Below us wound the ribbon of the road, with the two smudges that were our cars on the grass verge. On the other side the land rose steeply again and on the far horizon a group of houses stood like sentinels.

'One of those is Jill and David's,' I said, realising that this was in reverse the same view I had had from their house. And immediately all the worries I had put to one side washed over me again. I wondered uneasily how Nicholas would react to the knowledge that Jill and Barry Fenton were meeting secretly. To dispel such thoughts, I said hastily,

'What about your family? Are your parents still alive?'

'Unfortunately no. I just have a married brother who lives in Ireland. As a matter of fact I'm going over there tomorrow, to spend a few weeks with them.'

'I should think you'll be glad to get away. The school must seem very barren in the holidays.'

'It does rather. I have a small flat in the middle of the building, and it's a bit depressing being surrounded by long, empty corridors. During term-time we have about thirty boarders, and several of the masters live in the main building too, so there's certainly plenty going on then!'

'But surely, even with the masters, there's always a slight air of reserve, with your being the Head. You can't ever be really at your ease with each other.'

'I can with Robert. He and I were at Oxford together. He doesn't pull his punches, I assure you.'

'You've no real friends outside the school?'

'Not now. I suppose I was wrong to let things slide, but friendships need working at, and I simply haven't had the time to devote to them.'

I looked at him curiously. 'That school means an awful lot to you, doesn't it?'

'Yes,' he said slowly, his eyes on the distance, 'an awful lot. I've worked hard to get where I am, Christy, and in the process several things have gone by the board. I had to convince the powers-that-be that I was capable of holding the position. They tend to think that anyone under forty is a cheeky young upstart!'

'But now that you've realised your ambition—'

'I have to fight like mad to hold on to it. I've such a lot of plans for the school, if I can only bring them off.'

'What, for instance?'

'I won't bore you with all the details.'

'But I want to know.'

'Some of them are so nebulous I haven't even put them into words to myself.'

'Then try them out on me.'

He glanced sideways at me. 'They're also highly confidential.'

'Of course.'

'Well, I think the peak of my ambition is to get Manor House recognised as the official prep school for Highbury.'

'Phew! I'll say this for you, you aim high.'

'I think I can do it.'

'I'm sure you can.'

He looked at me sharply, suspecting mockery, but when he saw I was serious, he said simply, 'Thank you. I hope you're right. But that's one reason why I keep things on a pretty tight rein. The high level has to be maintained all the time, I just can't afford to let it slide for a moment. But as I said, that is very much between you and me.'

We stayed on our rock for some time, talking or not as the mood took us, until the sun moved round behind the trees and a faint cool breeze touched us.

Nicholas stood up and stretched. 'I don't know about you, but I'm beginning to feel hungry.'

'Yes, there is a limit to the sustenance in an egg and an apple.'

'Especially when they're half measures! Poor Christy! Come on, then, we'd better make a move.'

We retraced our steps through the little wood and down the hill to where Nicholas's jacket still guarded my painting equipment.

'We've surplus transport, haven't we?' he remarked as we reached the cars.

'You know, you don't really have to stand me dinner.'

'Getting cold feet?'

'No, but—'

'That was a condition of sharing your lunch. You can't get out of it now.'

'If you're sure, then—'

'I'm sure.'

'We'll have to go home our separate ways now, anyway.'

'Yes, I'll pick you up in an hour.'

I got in my own car and wound down all the windows. The heat was intense and the leather burned my bare legs. 'See you later, then.'

He raised his hand in a salute and I drove out on to the road. Michael last night, Nicholas tonight! I was not at all sure that I approved of myself, but the prospect of Nicholas's company during the evening ahead filled me with an excited expectancy which I had never felt for Michael.

I had just climbed out of the bath when the phone rang.

'Christy? Nicholas. Look, I just bumped into Val and she's issued a very pressing invitation for us to eat with them. How do you feel about it?'

'I'd love to.'

'Fine. I'll call for you about seven.'

'I'll be ready, but I must go now—I'm dripping on the carpet!'

I heard his laugh as I replaced the receiver.

It was one of those evenings which are a success from the beginning. Valerie was small, dark and vivacious, and my first favourable impression of her at Pamela's slid naturally into easy friendship. Robert was quieter, and I caught his eyes on me reflectively once or twice.

'You'll be glad to know, Val,' Nicholas remarked, 'that Christy has undertaken to "re-humanise" me!'

'"Re-humanise"? What a glorious word!'

'I didn't undertake any such thing!' I protested.

'You said I needed it, and I can't think of anyone better qualified to carry out the treatment! I'm more relaxed now than I've been for months—ask Val.'

'You'll have your hands full, Christy! These schoolmasters can get so *stuffy*!'

'*Thank* you, my love!' returned Robert drily.

She laughed at him. 'You know you do, but I admit Nicholas is even worse!'

'Thanks from me, too! Never mind, Val, at least you have an ally now.'

After the meal we sat a long time over coffee. I wondered if Lydia Marshbanks took part in many such evenings, and some of my contentment evaporated. David and Michael both said Nicholas was thinking of marrying her. I moved suddenly and Val asked,

'Are you cold? Close the window now, will you, Robert? It's almost dark.'

The evening ended at last and Robert and Valerie came out to see us into the car.

'It's been lovely,' I told them. 'Thank you so much.'

'You must come again.'

As we drew up outside the cottage, Nicholas remarked, 'It's been quite a day, hasn't it?'

'Quite a day.'

He came round and opened the car door for me and we walked slowly up the path.

'I'm off to Ireland tomorrow, but perhaps I can see you when I get back?'

'Yes, I'd like that. Goodnight, Nicholas, and thank you.'

'Goodnight. By the way—' he turned back, 'just how comprehensive is this course of yours? Is kissing part of the curriculum?'

I felt my breathing quicken. 'I rather think it's an optional extra.'

'Could I have a free sample, please?'

He made no move towards me. With his back to the street lamp, his face was completely in the shadow.

'Now?' I asked uncertainly.

'Now.'

I raised my hands and drew his head down to mine. His mouth was sweet and firm and strong. After a moment, I let my hands drop, but before I could move away, he caught hold of my face and held my mouth against his for long minutes more. At last we moved gently apart.

He said very softly, 'You realise you might be starting something you can't finish?'

'I don't think so.'

'In that case I'll take the complete course, including extras.'

He lifted his hand to touch my cheek. 'Goodnight, Christy!

'Goodnight.'

It wasn't till I had reached my bedroom that I realised my face was wet with tears.

CHAPTER SEVEN

The next day, August-like, the weather broke, and day after day of relentless rain fell. The village street moved with running water and only the ducks, strutting and preening on the village green, rejoiced in the change.

After two days of this a wild restlessness took hold of me. I paced round and round the studio like a caged animal while the rain rattled on the roof and sluiced down the windows. I couldn't settle to anything, and quite suddenly the smallness of the cottage, which normally I loved, closed in on me like a prison. There was nothing for it—I should have to go out. A walk in the rain might do me good.

I arrayed myself in mac and boots and opened the front door. As it closed behind me the phone started to ring. I hesitated. With Nicholas and Jill away it would probably be Michael, and he was the last person I felt I could face at the moment. I needed to be a lot more sure of myself before I saw Michael again. Ignoring the insistent ringing, I went on down the path.

That day set the pattern. As the rain continued, so did my restlessness, and day after day I set off to explore deserted lanes on the outskirts of the village. Once I went back to the field where Nicholas and I had shared our lunch and retraced our steps through the wood to the rock where we had sat. But a curtain of rain hung across the valley, hiding everything, and our rock was running with water. An appalling sense of melancholy swept over me, as though it were years rather than days since we had been here together, as though he would never come back to me. I turned and ran all the way back to the car.

But even after exhausting myself during the day, the evenings alone at the cottage grew unbearable. I became obsessed with the thought that Michael would phone or call round, and I didn't know what I could say to him. I started to go farther afield, lunching in deserted little pubs and often going on to a cinema afterwards so that I need not arrive home till bedtime. Even so, the phone was ringing several times as I opened the front door, which only confirmed my fears. I never answered it.

Altogether, it was a strange and frightening time. I had never experienced anything like this before, and I was distinctly worried that I had not been able to regain control of myself as I usually did.

After about a week, however, I had to answer the phone. It started to ring as I was standing at the door paying the milkman, and I could hardly ignore it. To my overwhelming relief, it was Val Temple.

'Christy, there's a Bring and Buy Sale at the church hall tomorrow morning, in aid of the church roof. I wondered if you'd like to come?'

'Oh, I would! I seem to have been living like a hermit since I saw you!'

'I know, it's this ghastly weather!'

'Ought I to bring something?'

'In theory, yes, but it doesn't matter that much.'

'What are you taking?'

'A cake and some scones and a jar or two of jam.'

'How domesticated! I think I'll cheat and just bring some bath-salts and tablets of soap.'

'That'll do fine.' She paused. 'Have you heard from Nicholas?'

'No, I didn't really expect to. Have you?'

'Just a brief scrawl to say the fishing was good.'

'I suppose that means it's raining there, too.'

'Very probably! See you tomorrow, then, about eleven.'

I replaced the receiver, picked up the milk bottles and went slowly through to the kitchen. It was true I hadn't expected to hear from Nicholas—but if he'd sent a card to the Temples, he might have sent me one too.

The church hall was across the road from St Barnabas, alongside the school, and was in fact frequently commandeered for school plays, concerts and speech days. I duly went over with my offerings of bath-salts and soap, and

103

the first person I saw, behind a stall directly opposite the door, was Lydia Marshbanks. As I stood hesitating and trying to find Val, a girl at the next stall called across,

'Are you coming to the Cricket Club hop, Lydia?'

She turned, pushing her long hair off her face. 'No, Nick's in Ireland. He's having ghastly weather, poor darling, but he seems happy enough, splashing about in the bogs!'

Under cover of the laughter which greeted this comment, all the dreams I had been building during my long, solitary walks came crashing down round my head. So he had written to her, too. Well, he would, wouldn't he? After all, he was going to marry her — everyone said so. Had I really imagined that a few hours could change all those long-term plans?

Behind me, Val's voice said, 'Hello, sorry I'm late!' and a completely instinctive sense of self-preservation instantly took over. At least I could make sure that no one, and least of all Val, should know what an abysmal fool I had made of myself. My smile, I felt sure, was completely natural, though I thought she looked at me a little oddly.

'Come and deposit your goodies on the appropriate stall. I think toilet things are down there. Just hang on a sec, will you, while I unload mine on to Lydia.'

Unwillingly, but still smiling brightly, I

followed her across the hall.

'Hello, Val! Scones—oh, gorgeous! Thanks!'

'By the way, do you two know each other?'

Lydia's eyes held mine, long and green and challenging. 'I think I've seen you around,' she said carelessly.

'Christy—Lydia.'

We nodded at each other and Lydia opened a box Val had handed her.

'Oh, bless you, Val! You've brought one of those heavenly gateaux we had at half-term! Pity Nick won't be able to sample this one!'

Valerie said steadily, 'I should slice it if I were you—most people would find it a bit rich to buy whole. Will you excuse us, Lydia, Christy had better get her things on the stall.'

She took my arm and led me down the hall. I seemed to stand apart from myself, watching as if at a theatre my gay talk with Val and the others, while all the time the hard, tight knot of agony inside was swelling to fill the emptiness. Would I never learn? Oh, fool, fool, to place so much importance on a couple of kisses!

Val was speaking and I wrenched my attention back to her.

'I said, would you like a cup of coffee?'

'Oh—sorry, Val. Yes, please.'

'Look,' she said awkwardly, 'you don't want to take too much notice of Lydia, you know.'

'Lydia?' I repeated stupidly, my panic-stricken brain registering that my performance couldn't have been as convincing as I'd hoped. 'Oh, you mean Nicholas's girl-friend. How do you mean, take too much notice?'

I swallowed down the scalding coffee. Val was staring at me, but as I met her eyes she looked away and said flatly, 'Nothing. It doesn't matter.'

It was then that I caught sight of Liz Bannister, and so completely upside-down was my world at that moment that I completely forgot I had spent the last ten days trying to avoid her father, and almost ran across the room towards her, pulling Val with me.

Liz, bless her, unknowingly played right into my hands. 'Hello, Christy! I was hoping you'd be here. I've strict instructions to invite you for supper tonight and to take no refusals. And I happen to know Father has tickets for the new play on Saturday, so you'd better write that in your diary at the same time! Look what I've got!' She held up a scarf about four feet long. 'That'll slay them at Oxford, won't it?'

'Sure to!' I said out of a dry mouth. I was acutely conscious of Val's stiffness at my side. Liz had turned to her.

'How's Diana Fenton, Mrs Temple? I heard she wasn't too good at the end of term.'

'No, she wasn't. They're away at the moment, of course. I hope the change does her good. She's quite a long way to go yet.'

'Yes. Well, I must fly, or Dad won't be getting any lunch! About seven, Christy?'

106

'Lovely!'

To hell with Nicholas! I turned to Val with a bright smile. 'Shall we go and have a look at those cactus plants? They'd look rather good on my kitchen windowsill.'

We had an outwardly gay evening at the Bannisters'. Liz got out her record player and we all sat on the floor drinking shandy and listening to the rain when the music stopped. It occurred to me that I could do a lot worse than commit myself to many more such evenings. But when Liz went out of the room to make coffee, Michael pulled me gently over against him and said against my hair,

'I've missed you, Christy. I phoned several times, but you were never in.'

'The rain made me restless. I've been walking around in it like a lost soul!' But a happy lost soul, then.

'I thought perhaps you were avoiding me. Did Liz tell you about the theatre? You will come, won't you?'

I stirred unhappily. 'Michael, you do realise—'

'No strings?'

'Yes.'

'Very well, if you insist.'

Liz came back. I would have moved, but Michael's arm tightened slightly. She said easily, 'It's all right, Christy, stay there—I'll pour.'

That night I lay in bed and considered

coldly and calculatingly whether or not I should marry Michael. He wasn't, after all, as weak as David—I'd been too hasty in my comparison. He was kind and good and 'a very present help in trouble'. The words came unbidden into my mind. That was the crux of it. I hurled myself over, buried my face in the pillow, and cried as if my heart would break.

*   *   *

September dawned, clouded, overcast and warm, and one morning Jill phoned.

'Hello, Christy, how are things? Just thought I'd let you know we're back.'

'Did you have a good holiday?' I daren't be more explicit.

'Oh, not so bad. The weather was a bit mixed. It was a rest anyway, and the boys enjoyed it.'

'It will have done you good.'

'I hope so. What have you been doing with yourself?'

'Oh—walking—going to bring and buy sales—a concert and the theatre.'

'With Michael?'

'Yes.'

'You must bring him round to dinner one night.'

'Thanks.'

'I can't come over today—the car really is being serviced!' Her words brought back my attempts to keep her away from the school. 'Can you come here instead?'

'Not today, I'm afraid. I have to go into Gloucester to restock with paints. Tomorrow, if you're free?'

'Lovely. Come for lunch.'

It was starting to rain again after lunch as I went through the garden to the garage. The engine spluttered, missed on two cylinders, and died. Nothing that I tried revived it. Blast! That meant I'd have to go by bus. I hadn't time to wait for the mechanic to come out, and Jill couldn't help since her own car was out of action too. Dejectedly I pulled a scarf over my head and trudged back through the garden out on to the High Street to the bus stop. The rain came on heavier, dripping down my neck. I was so huddled into myself that I didn't notice a car had stopped beside me until the door opened and Nicholas's voice said curtly, 'Get in!'

I stared at him blankly.

'Get in, for heaven's sake. What on earth are you doing there?'

'Waiting for a bus,' I snapped, needled by his tone. 'I should have thought it was obvious.'

'Where do you want to go?'

'Gloucester.'

'I'll take you.'

There's no need. I can easily—'

'Stop being so damned independent. I'm on

109

my way there anyway.'

I bit my lip furiously. This was certainly different from the atmosphere in which we'd last parted. The car leapt forward and I pulled off my headscarf and shook out my hair.

'I was under the impression that you were still waist-high in some Irish bog.' My tone implied that it was a pity he wasn't.

'I'd had enough of the rain, so I came back.'

'It's no better here.'

'So I see.'

I glanced sideways at him. His face was hard and set. Something had obviously annoyed him. We were back to square one again. I said acidly,

'Thanks for all the postcards.'

'Don't mention it.'

We sat in prickly silence for a couple more miles. Then I asked, 'What happened? Did all your rabbits die?'

He gave a short laugh. 'You might say that.'

'You're certainly—de-humanised again!'

'Yes. All in all I find I like it better that way.'

The brush-off, if ever there was one. Come and get him, Lydia, he's all yours!

'If you like,' I offered after a while, 'I could sing a verse or two of "Fight the Good Fight". It would help to pass the time.'

'Kind of you, but we're almost there.'

We were in fact on the outskirts of Gloucester.

'Whereabouts do you want to be?'

110

'That's the shop I'm going to, just along there. This will do fine.'

'Will you be long?'

'No, I've only got to collect some paints. Thanks for the lift.'

'I'll wait here for you.'

'Oh no, it's all right, I'll get the bus back.'

'Will you for God's sake do what you're told for once?'

'It doesn't seem to occur to you,' I flashed, 'that I might not *want* your company for another twenty minutes on the way home!'

'I should have thought it was preferable to waiting for a bus in the rain.'

'Not to me, it isn't!'

We glared at each other, then he smiled crookedly. 'Damn you, you give as good as you get, don't you? All right, I grant you I've been something less than my usual charming self this afternoon, but having brought you here I have every intention of taking you back again, so you might as well resign yourself to the fact. There's a free meter here.'

'What about the things you want to get yourself?'

'Go and buy your paints, girl!'

I caught up my scarf and flounced out of the car. The effect was somewhat spoilt by the fact that I landed in a puddle. Tears of mortification and disappointment were stinging my eyes. What had happened to the fragile, tender thing that had been blossoming

111

between us at our last meeting? Had it really only been my imagination? I caught sight of my reflection in a mirror behind the art counter and for the first time saw a resemblance to Jill, as she looked when I'd tried to lecture her about Barry: rebellious eyes and full, sulky mouth. I sorted out the tubes I wanted, the Letraset and the paper, paid the assistant and hurried out. Nicholas was sitting smoking in the car with the radio on.

'Put your things on the back seat. We're going for a cup of tea.'

'Why?'

'Because I'm thirsty. Also, I'm not going to waste the money I put in the meter. And,' he continued evenly, without looking at me, 'if you mention that bloody bus again, I'll put you across my knee and spank you, so help me!'

Meekly I put my parcels where he directed and let him lead me over to the café. It occurred to me that perhaps I wasn't used to people standing up to me, either, in which case it should prove a salutary lesson for both of us.

'Now,' he said pleasantly, as we settled at a table, 'are you in a better temper?'

'I?' Words failed me.

'Because if so, there's a film I'd like to see at the Odeon.'

'I presume I've no choice in the matter?'

'Correct.'

'Damn you, Nicholas,' I said softly.

112

'That's better. Pot of tea for two and two toasted tea-cakes, please.'

I looked smoulderingly across at him. The Irish weather had browned his skin, even if there had been no sunshine. I wondered helplessly what the point of all this was. If he regretted the day we had spent together, the easiest thing would be to avoid me now, rather than force me to spend hours in his company. Or was he simply trying to make it quite clear that what was past was past and that our old back-biting relationship was the one which he intended to pursue in future?

'If you've finished your tea, I believe the film starts at five.'

Silently I fastened my coat and we went out together into the rain.

It was a war film, and the shriek of crashing planes and deafening bursts of gunfire exploded through my head with an exquisite agony. I sat stiffly beside Nicholas, my glazed eyes fixed on the flickering screen. Never, I resolved, would I go anywhere with him again—never!

It was a long film, over two hours. As it finished, Nicholas said, 'Do you want to stay for the second feature?'

'No, thank you.'

'Sure?'

'Quite sure.'

The rain was as unremitting as ever. We drove home in almost total silence.

'Thank you,' I said stiffly, as the car stopped at the cottage gate.

'On the whole, it was nobly borne.'

I said coldly, 'Don't get out.'

'All right. Remember me to friend Bannister.'

I slammed the door, and in the same instant the car leapt forward, spraying me with muddy water. I started to laugh hysterically. Of all the horrible, miserable, beastly days—

The telephone rang as I opened the front door. I lifted it to hear Michael's voice. I said weakly,

'Oh, Michael!' and to my horror burst into tears.

'Christy! My darling girl, what is it? Aren't you well?'

Furiously I tried to control my breathing. 'I'm sorry—I've just got the most splitting headache.'

'Shall I come round? Can I do anything?'

'No, I think I'll just go straight to bed.'

'It's no use suggesting the cinema, then?'

The hysterical laughter welled again and I bit it back. 'No, frankly, I'm afraid it isn't.'

'Take a couple of aspirins or something and I'll phone in the morning to see how you are.'

Shakily I went through to the living-room, surprised to find it was not yet eight o'clock. It was then that I realised I had left all the supplies I had bought on the back seat of Nicholas's car. And in the same moment, the doorbell rang. He must have found them as soon as he got home. But I *couldn't* let him see me all tear-stained and dishevelled.

The bell rang again, imperiously. I had no choice. He knew I was in. I took a deep breath and flung open the door.

He began: 'I thought you might be needing—' and broke off.

I didn't look at him. I reached blindly for the parcels, said indistinctly, 'Thank you' and quickly shut the door. Safe on the inside I stood immobile, clutching the packages. It seemed a very long time before I heard him turn and walk slowly back down the path.

CHAPTER EIGHT

It didn't take long, the next morning, for the garage mechanic to fix the car, and then, still with the after-effects of one of the worst headaches of my life, I drove round to Jill's. She looked very bronzed and well, but her eyes kept sliding away from mine. I asked no questions. I was having too much trouble with my own problems to attempt to solve hers. The boys were as exuberant as puppies, rushing in and out of the door until my vision blurred.

'Thank God it's school next week!' their mother said fervently. 'The summer holidays are never-ending.'

'How's David?'

'Well,' she answered briefly. She stood up and searched in her bag for cigarettes. 'I'm glad you've been seeing Michael, Christy. Do you think he'd make up a party with us to go to the Golf Club dance? It's the first of the season, at the Shipton.'

'I don't think dances are much in my line these days.'

'Rubbish! You talk like an old maid!'

'I am one,' I said succinctly.

She flushed. 'I'm sorry, I didn't mean that. But don't let yourself be old before your time. After all, we're only young once.' Her voice shook inexplicably and she drew deeply on her cigarette. 'Will you come, if I ask him? It's on Friday.'

'All right.'

'We could have dinner here first. Then next week I'm trying to organise two tables of bridge for the Conservative Club. Are you available for that?'

'No, count me out of that, Jill. I haven't time to indulge in such a round of social occasions. I'm a working girl, remember.'

The boys were with us for lunch, of course, and talk was general, for which I was grateful. I wasn't up to any tête-à-têtes with Jill at the moment. Nor did I accept her invitation to stay for supper. I hadn't slept well the previous night and intended to have an early night.

I heard the phone ringing as I came round the house, but it had stopped by the time I opened the door. It was probably Michael checking that my headache had gone. I wondered whether to phone him back, but couldn't be bothered and went straight to bed.

On the Friday evening, Michael called for me as arranged and we went round to Jill and David's for dinner. Pamela and Harry were there, and another couple, Hazel and Dick, whom I'd met several times before.

Jill always excelled herself on such occasions, and the cold buffet laid out in the dining room appealed to my artistic eye almost as much as to my palate. Yet despite its attraction, I had little appetite. I was very much aware that Nicholas would be at the dance, and I was not looking forward to seeing him again. Nor would that be the only tension of the evening; Barry Fenton was also likely to be there. I wondered if anyone else had noticed that Jill's laugh was just a little too high, her face a little too flushed. I saw David's eyes on her, and knew he was bracing himself for their inevitable meeting. Had he been able, in Dorset, to pull her back, or not?

Michael said, 'You're very quiet tonight, Christy!

'Sorry!'

'I don't mind, as long as nothing's wrong?'

'To be honest, I'm not really in the mood for a dance tonight.'

'We needn't go, you know.'

'Oh yes, we need! Jill would never forgive me if I backed out now.'

I laid down my plate with the last of the gateau pushed to one side, and Jill called brightly,

'Has everyone finished? We might as well go, then.'

David was standing in the hall as Michael and I went out to the car. I pressed his hand reassuringly and he gave me a brief smile. There was no denying, I thought ruefully as I sat back in Michael's car, that life was a lot less wearing in Bournemouth!

The ballroom at the Shipton Court had a

bar through an archway at one end, and chairs and tables round the floor. We all congregated at one table, joined by several more of Jill and David's friends. I was careful not to let my eyes go round the ballroom. If Nicholas was here there was nothing I could do about it, but I certainly was not going to look for him. Then, as luck would have it, he stopped opposite me in the Paul Jones.

'Good evening,' he said formally.

'Good evening.'

I made no attempt whatsoever at conversation, and we circled slowly in a slow waltz.

'It's a good floor, isn't it?' he remarked after a moment.

I looked up, but he met my eyes without a tremor.

'Very.'

'Do you come here often?'

He was deliberately going through all the most hackneyed opening gambits of the dance floor. I said seriously,

'Actually, I prefer the Palais.'

'Quite so.' There was a ghost of a twitch at the corner of his mouth. 'And how's your Yorkshire grandmother these days?'

That was the first allusion he had made to our magical day, and it took me all my time to keep my voice steady.

'She's in Strangeways, I'm sorry to say.'

'So they finally caught up with her! Too

bad.'

The music changed, he gave me a little bow, and we were swept into our respective circles. I didn't see him again, but later in the evening, as I danced with Harry Towers, I did see Jill and Barry Fenton very close together in a dark corner, and my spirits sank to rock bottom. When David in turn asked me to dance, I took the bull by the horns.

'How are things?'

'Pretty bloody.'

'Oh, David!'

'She tried—I'll give her that. I just had the impression that every time I touched her, she was wishing it was him.' His eyes were bleak. 'Anyway, short of leaving the village altogether, there's nothing more that I can do. If they want to meet now, I can't stop them.'

'If you do think of leaving the village let me know—I'll join you!'

'You! But I thought you loved it! You're not sorry you came already, are you?'

'I suppose not. I still love it. It's the people in it that take a bit of getting used to!'

'Michael? He's serious, isn't he?'

'I'm afraid so.'

'It's no good?'

'No.'

'A pity. I like him, and he's had a raw deal.'

'I know. I'm sorry too.'

At the end of that dance I excused myself and escaped to the cloakroom, wondering how soon I could decently suggest going home. Valerie Temple was just turning away from a dressing-table and we almost collided.

'Hello, Val. Did you ever hear how much they made at the sale?'

'Oh—hello, Christy.' Her eyes dropped. 'Yes, it was quite a success, I believe. Excuse me, Robert's waiting.'

She moved past me and hurried out of the door, leaving me staring after her. I'd thought I had a friend in Val, quite apart from her association with Nicholas. Obviously I was mistaken. The unpleasant little encounter was just one more reason why I did not enjoy myself that evening. I was supremely thankful when at last it was time to go and there was no risk of being snubbed by anyone else. It would be a long time before Jill talked me into going to any more dances.

And yet, when at last I was in bed, sleep would not come. My feet were aching from all the unaccustomed dancing, and behind my closed eyes the crowds still moved in time to the music. For the hundredth time I went over in my mind all my meetings with Nicholas, searching in vain for some reason for his complete volte-face. What could I have possibly done to have blotted my copybook so thoroughly that after our wonderful day together he should not only write to Lydia and Val from Ireland without a line to me, but should subject me to such open hostility at our next meeting? His last words that evening had seemed to indicate that he meant our closeness to continue: 'You may be starting something you can't finish' and, after my reassurance, 'Then I'll take the full course, including extras.' Those were the sentences which had been the cornerstone for all my castle-building during those long wet days.

I realised that I was lying rigid, with jaw tensed and hands clenched, and forced myself to relax. My relationship with Nicholas had all the uncertainty of a child blowing at dandelions: 'He loves me—he don't.' And I seemed to have run out of dandelions.

*   *   *

The weeks passed. I worked hard on a new batch of designs, and was glad to relax in Michael's company from time to time. He was being careful to make no demands on me, and I was grateful. I had seen very little of Jill since the dance, and that suited me too. But one morning in early October I saw her car stop at the gate and knew with a sinking heart that I could no longer shut myself away from her problems.

I leant out of the studio window as she came up the path.

'Let yourself in, will you, Jill, the door's on the latch. I've a rather tricky piece of artwork I can't leave for the moment.'

She lifted a hand in acknowledgement and a moment later I heard her feet on the stairs.

'You don't mind if I go on working, do you?'

'No, carry on.'

'When I've finished this bit we can have a cup of coffee.'

She watched me for a moment or two, then moved restlessly away, picking up canvases that were stacked against the wall, fiddling with folders and the trolley of paints until I wanted to scream. At last, from the far end of the studio, she said abruptly,

'It's no good, you know, Christy.'

'What isn't?' I was stalling for time as I carefully glued the minute illustrations on to the card.

'About Barry. I'm not going to get over it. I can't. It's too late for that.'

I was thankful that the preciseness of my work didn't allow me to look up. 'What are you going to do, then?'

'I don't know.' She started to walk aimlessly about again. 'Every time we see each other, it's worse.'

'There's an obvious remedy for that.'

'I suppose so. The point is, I don't want to stop seeing him. And he feels the same. He told me.'

'When?'

'Oh, in one of the snatched moments we had together. That's what's so damnable, we can never meet in a place this size without being seen by someone we know. And we've got to talk, Christy. We've just got to. There's so much to try to work out.'

'I'll tell you one thing,' I said caustically, my face a couple of inches above the surface of the desk, 'so just take warning. He won't do anything to jeopardise his career, and you'd better accept the fact. Over-sexed he might be, but he's ambitious too.'

'Christy! Don't be so vile!'

'I just want you to look at it with your eyes open, that's all. He may be only too ready for a bit of fun while his wife's *hors de combat*, so to speak, but that school's a wonderful jumping-off place. If he can give it as a reference, there's no limit to the positions that will be open to him in the future.'

She smiled wryly. 'You forget you're preaching to the converted, as far as the school is concerned. I didn't know you were championing it these days, as well.'

'I'm not, I'm merely saying don't burn your boats or you'll be left high and dry. Which, even if a mixed metaphor, is still an applicable one.'

'All right, so you don't approve. I didn't expect you to. But you will help us, won't you?'

'Help you?' In my surprise I smudged the glue and swore softly under my breath. 'How in the name of goodness can I help? Even if I wanted to?'

'By letting us meet here occasionally. Now

listen—' she went on quickly at my indignant protest—'hear me out before you have apoplexy! I told you we *have* to meet. You must see that. And we obviously can't meet anywhere around Biddleton. You probably know that David saw us once before. And since Barry's only free time is between three and four a couple of afternoons a week, we haven't time to go further afield. I can't see him at home—it's too open, for one thing, and of course there's Ginette. But this cottage would be ideal. We could use the lane and come across the garden, and no one would be any the wiser.'

'Except me,' I said grimly. 'No!'

'But, Christy, be reasonable! I'm sure you want this settled one way or the other almost as much as I do. It wouldn't put you out in any way. You could just leave the garden door open and I'd come and wait. If he couldn't make it I'd go quietly away again, and if he could—well, we'd have a chance to talk it all out and at least know where we stand.'

'And what am I supposed to do? Play gooseberry or clear off every afternoon and leave you the run of the place?'

'Neither,' she said patiently. 'Just stay up here working, as you would anyway.'

'I don't like it, Jill, it's too risky. I don't want any part of your philanderings.'

'But I just explained that it isn't risky at all! And it's only a couple of times a week, when the boys have games. He'd have to be back in time to supervise them going home, and of course I'd have to be there to collect Tim, too. Ginette could go for Mark at half-past three. Please, Christy, please—you're our only hope!'

'No. I'm sorry, but no.'

She collapsed like a burst balloon—literally collapsed, sinking down on a chair with her flimsy dress billowing out about her and tears pouring down her face.

'Oh, for God's sake!' I said irritably, pushing my work away. Jill could even cry prettily, an accomplishment I'd envied her all our lives. 'Can't you even begin to see it my way? You say I'm your only hope. So if I *don't* help you, it will have to fizzle out, which is the best thing that could happen.'

'But I love him!' she sobbed. 'It's all very well for you, you don't know what it's like! And it won't stop us seeing each other anyway, because if the only way we can see each other is by taking risks, then we'll have to take them, and that way David is far more likely to get hurt, if that's what's worrying you.'

I said slowly, 'How long do you propose this should go on? Two afternoons a week for ever more?'

She looked up, sensing that I was weakening. I would defy anyone to resist Jill's tears.

'No, only for a week or two, until we can decide the best thing to do.'

'Jill, you *know* the best thing already.'

She looked at me piteously, huge eyes swimming.

I said abruptly, 'There would have to be a definite limit. After all, it shouldn't take long to thrash out.'

'We'd only have about forty-five minutes, you know, allowing time for travelling. Oh, Christy, bless you! You will help, won't you?'

Still I hesitated. 'I really don't think—'

She jumped up. 'It's the only chance we have of coming to any lasting decision. What use do you think I am to David while this is going on? It's for his sake as well as ours.'

'What afternoons are they?'

'Tuesdays and Thursdays. Oh, thank you, darling! You'll hardly know we're here, I promise. Can I tell him it's all right for tomorrow?'

'I suppose so,' I said heavily, 'but for two weeks only. After that, you're on your own.'

She wasn't listening. 'The garden door doesn't stay open by itself, does it?'

'I'll prop it open for you. I can't give you the key, I need it myself.'

'Christy, I can't thank you enough!' She dropped a kiss on top of my bent head. 'I'll go now and let you get on with your work. Goodbye, darling—you won't regret it, really!'

'I certainly hope not.'

She clattered happily down the stairs and the front door closed behind her. Well, I'd committed myself now, and despite her wheedling I still felt like a traitor. How I could face David, or, for that matter, Nicholas? I reminded myself sharply that my allegiance to my sister was greater than any I owed to him, that, in fact, Nicholas Blair had no claim to my loyalty at all. On which sour note I returned to my work.

Despite Jill's bland reassurances, I couldn't work the next afternoon. I sat miserably tense up in the studio with my eyes on the clock, longing for the time for them to be gone, wondering if anyone had seen them slip in, or would see them go. I must have been mad to agree to these assignations. At last I heard the living room door open and the murmur of voices. Then Jill called up softly,

'Goodbye, Christy! Thank you for having us!'

I let out my breath in a long sigh of relief. That was one over; only three more to go. But it wasn't quite as simple as that.

At half-past three the following Tuesday, Jill suddenly shrieked up the stairs,

'Christy! Mr Blair's car's stopped at the gate! For God's sake get rid of him!'

I jumped up, knocking over a tin of paint, and without conscious thought ran straight downstairs and out on to the path. The day was cool and cloudy, and I was immediately aware of my bare arms. At the gate, Nicholas paused in surprise at my headlong approach.

'Is this impetuous welcome for me?'

'No, I—oh, hello!' I stopped, feeling acutely foolish.

He raised an eyebrow. 'Hello,' he replied patiently. 'I wonder if you could spare me a few minutes? There's something I want to discuss with you.'

'What?'

'We can hardly talk here, surely. You're shivering already. Can we go inside for a minute?'

'I—I was just going out, actually.'

'Without a coat?'

'Only down to the baker's.'

'Can't it wait?'

'Not really,' I said miserably.

Nicholas studied my face. 'You don't want me to go inside, do you? Why not?'

'It's not that, I—'

'It most certainly is that.' His eyes glinted with curiosity. 'Who have you got holed up in there? Did Grandma make a break from Strangeways?'

I didn't reply. I would never forgive Jill for putting me in this ludicrous position.

He said shortly, 'All right, I'm not going to force an entry. If we can't talk here, we'll obviously have to go somewhere else. Get in the car.'

There was nothing else to do. A moment later we were driving down the High Street, and as we swung round over the bridge

Nicholas said abruptly,

'It was Bannister, wasn't it?'

I turned to stare at him. 'What was?'

'Whom you didn't want me to meet.'

'Why on earth should I care if you meet Michael? But if he *had* been there—which he wasn't—I would hardly have come out with you, would I?'

His foot went down hard on the accelerator. 'Of course not. Stupid of me. Just a touch of the usual megalomania.'

It had happened again. Every time we met now, something sparked off this barbed hostility. Damn Jill and her schemings; this time it was her fault.

'What did you want to discuss with me?' I asked tentatively, hoping to regain safer ground.

'I wanted some professional advice.'

'Oh?'

A sudden spurt of rain rattled on the windscreen. When he didn't elucidate, I said, 'Where are we going?'

'To the Art Gallery.'

I bit back my surprise. Questions only seemed to irritate him when he was driving.

It was raining quite heavily by the time we parked the car. Nicholas took off his jacket and handed it to me. 'Put this round your shoulders.'

'I'm all right—'

'Do you never,' he asked heavily, 'do

anything without arguing?'

He took my elbow as we hurried up the wide steps, his hand warm on my cool arm.

'It's the first floor we want.'

He led me into one of the smaller rooms.

'Now—look at that.'

I don't know what I had expected, but he had indicated an extremely long canvas, depicting, as far as I could judge at a quick glance, a series of medieval battles—knights in armour, ladies in pointed hats watching from balconies, surprised-looking horses.

'All right, I've looked at it.'

I turned my head, surprising a strangely contemplative expression in his eyes. They shuttered over as they met mine.

'Could you design me something like that?'

'What on earth for?'

'The third form boys are embarking on the ancient history of the Cotswolds—you know, Celts and Normans and all the rest of it, up to the present day. It'll bring in a lot about the Tudors, of course, and the Churchills at Blenheim, and so on. I thought it might be an idea to have a kind of visual link connected with their art—a kind of Bayeux Tapestry, in fact. It could be done in separate sections of a given length, and they could copy the appropriate one, in paints or possibly as a collage, whichever appealed to them.' His eyes twinkled briefly. 'To encourage self-expression, of course. And by the end of the project, they should have quite a clear picture of the times—the historical costumes, the Stately Homes, the battles, and so on. What do you think?'

'I think it would be fascinating,' I said slowly, 'but it would be an incredibly big undertaking.'

'I realise that. There'd have to be a lot of research before you could even start. I've quite a collection of books on the subject, which, of course, you could have free access to, and since I'd be employing your services professionally, I would naturally agree to whatever fee you feel would be suitable.'

'But what about your own art mistress? Couldn't she do it for you?'

'Confidentially, I'm not quite as confident of her abilities as I was.'

I looked at him quickly. 'I hope to goodness it wasn't anything I said. I was just being supercritical because I was annoyed with Jill at the time. I certainly didn't mean—'

'No, it's not that. Or not only. There have been one or two occasions when I've felt she was not quite up to standard. As a matter of fact, I'm replacing her at the end of this term, and since this will be a fairly long-term thing, I felt it would be better in your hands.'

I looked again at the painting, and already my imagination was stirring. It would be completely engrossing once I started, I realised that. Ever since I'd come to Biddleton

I had been collecting odd snippets of history and folklore. They could all be woven into this. And more—very much more—it meant a lot of close contact with Nicholas. He must realise that.

'What do you say? Will you consider it?'

I turned to him, my face glowing with excitement. He drew in his breath sharply. 'Christy—'

And from across the gallery, like an unwelcome echo, came another voice:

'Christy! I thought it was you! What are you doing here?'

It was Michael. At my side, Nicholas said distinctly, 'Hell's teeth!'

Michael came quickly round the pillar which had hidden Nicholas from his sight, and, on seeing him, stopped dead.

'Oh, I beg your pardon. I thought you were alone.' He looked from one of us to the other in a rather bewildered way, and I realised that although Nicholas was fully aware of my association with Michael, he in fact knew nothing of my relationship—if it warranted the name—with Nicholas.

I said quickly, 'Nicholas has an idea for a historical design for me to work on. We've just come to look at this as a guide.'

'I see. I must admit I simply dashed in out of the rain! I've been going round a property for a client.'

He paused. 'Perhaps you'd both like to join

me for a cup of tea?'

'We'd rather not, if you don't mind,' Nicholas said pleasantly. 'We've rather a lot of things to discuss, and we'll be having an early dinner anyway.'

Michael's surprise equalled my own at this revelation.

'I see,' he said again, a little stiffly. 'Well, I'm sorry I interrupted you. I'll see you on Saturday, Christy.' He walked quickly away. I hoped fervently that the last remark hadn't registered.

'That,' I said reproachfully, 'was rather rude, wasn't it?'

'On the contrary, I was politeness itself.'

'Why did you tell him we were eating early?'

'Because we are. Concentration makes me hungry, and unless you'd like to sit and watch while I eat an enjoyable meal, you might as well join me. What happy little plans have you got for Saturday?'

I sighed. I should have known nothing escaped Nicholas.

'I don't know yet.'

'He seemed very sure of seeing you.'

'He usually does, on a Saturday.'

Yet another possible drawing together had been arrested. He said briskly, 'You still haven't said if you'll do this.'

'I'd like to try.'

'Good. Then let's have a drink to celebrate, before that early dinner.'

During that drink and dinner, he was polite and charming and a hundred miles away. We might have been two strangers who had happened to sit at the same table. My thoughts towards poor Michael would have startled him, to say the least. Not until the coffee arrived did he become the least personal, and then, being Nicholas, he went in with both feet.

'They're saying in the village that you're going to marry him.'

We had just been having an involved discussion on, of all things, modern Greek, and I must have jumped.

'Really?' I said, rushing my defences into position. 'Do let me know when you have a definite date.'

'Is it true?'

'Is it any business of yours?'

'None, I'm just curious. You don't deny, then, that he's asked you?'

I met his eye squarely. 'No, I don't deny it.'

His mouth tightened ominously.

'You must forgive my interest—it's just that I'm thinking of taking the same step myself.'

There was a brief, fathomless silence. My heart plummeted into it like a rock and disappeared without trace. For the life of me, I couldn't marshal my stiff lips to make any reply.

'No merry quips?' he asked tightly.

I said with an effort, 'Only congratulations,

135

if they're in order.'

'Possibly a little previous. I'm not quite so precipitate as friend Bannister.'

I said aridly, 'It's not exactly a surprise, of course. They've been saying *that* in the village ever since I came.'

'No doubt. It's been in my mind for quite some time.'

I said—and it was a continuing wonder to me that I could speak at all—

'Do you love her?'

I was looking down at the table, and I saw his knuckles whiten.

'We're compatible,' he replied in a clipped voice. 'There are a lot of things to take into account in a marriage, and love is only one of them.'

Something snapped inside me. 'I can't say I envy her! "Compatible", indeed! She might as well marry a computer!'

His voice shook. 'Obviously I don't measure up to the romantic standards of your intended!'

'Obviously.' I was fighting to control the fit of trembling that had seized me.

'I presume you *love* Bannister?'

I said clearly, 'I would never marry a man I didn't.'

His chair grated as he pushed it back from the table. 'There doesn't seem to be much point in prolonging the discussion. If you've finished, we might as well go.'

I hadn't finished, but I didn't care. Blindly I followed him out into the premature darkness of the wet evening. I would have to summon every ounce of control to enable me to survive the inescapable intimacy of the journey home. Thankfully, my groping mind fastened on a long library book I'd just finished. The moment we were in the car, I began.

'I've just been reading a most fascinating book, "The Knights of St George". Have you read it?'

'I thought it was a wine,' said Nicholas woodenly.

I couldn't believe he was attempting a joke, so I rushed on.

'The "k" kind of knights—all about the Crusades. I've always been a bit conservative in choosing historical novels and avoided anything pre-Tudor, though I could probably write a book myself on the Stuarts and the Civil War. I used to think anything further back was a bit too remote, somehow, but now I realise what I've been missing. Do you know much about the Plantagenets?'

'I did a paper on them once.'

'Oh, of course. I was forgetting. You read history at Oxford, didn't you? Which is your favourite period?'

'I've no idea,' said Nicholas unhelpfully.

I waited a moment, but he didn't elaborate. 'It was incredible, the debauchery and sheer inhumanity the Crusaders indulged in, in the name of Christianity. They used to set out across the desert intent on destroying a whole city, just because they considered its ruler an "infidel". And the lives of the poor people, who lived along the walls—it was unbelievably awful.'

I paused and glanced at him. His face was set and hard, his eyes on the wet road ahead.

'Jerusalem was always the prize, of course, even then. I wonder if any other city has been responsible for more bloodshed?'

I made a mental note not to finish my sentences on a question. Obviously no replies were forthcoming. I thought a little hysterically, 'I deserve an Oscar for this!'

'Anyway, it was a fabulous book. I believe there's a sequel—I must try to get hold of it. Not that I seem to have much time for reading these days.'

My voice faded into silence. I hoped that last comment hadn't been construed as meaning that all my spare time was spent with Michael. Not that it really made any difference now one way or the other how he took it. Thank heaven we were just turning the corner by the duckpond. I had done it.

He drew up outside the cottage and I said brightly, 'Thanks for the meal. I'll start thinking about the frieze and let you know any ideas that crop up.'

His hands were still gripping the wheel. He said slowly,

138

'For your information, you have the distinction of being quite the most infuriating woman I've ever met.'

'Thank you,' I said uncertainly.

'I'd give a lot to see you ruffled, just for once. Do you know that?'

I stared speechlessly down at my clasped hands. My performance must have been even better than I'd thought.

'Look at me when I'm talking to you!' he commanded harshly, for all the world as though I were one of his small boys. The ghost of a smile touched my mouth.

'Yes, sir!' I said, obediently turning my head.

'Damn you!' he said softly. 'Damn you, damn you, damn you!' He reached out suddenly and pulled me against him. It wasn't at all like the sweet tenderness of last time; it was a ruthless, passionate, self-gratifying kiss, and I gave myself up gladly to the onslaught of it. It seemed to go on for a long time, and we were both trembling at the end of it. We looked at each other for a long minute, then he said unsteadily,

'I think you'd better go.'

My hands were shaking so much I needed both of them to get the car door open. I'd meant to say goodnight, but I didn't seem able to speak. I just pushed the door to and immediately the car moved away up the road. Under the trembling there was a kind of wild, singing happiness. We had thought each other detached, and in the last few minutes we had both discovered otherwise.

I could hardly get the key into the lock, but at last I was inside. Propped up on the shelf by the telephone was a scrawled note from Jill. It read: 'Thanks, Christy, you're a pal! Will call tomorrow.'

I stared at it uncomprehendingly. I had forgotten all about her.

CHAPTER NINE

Jill came the next morning, on her way home from school.

'Gosh, that was a close one!' she began immediately. 'How did you manage to get him away?'

'Only by making a complete fool of myself. It was just the kind of thing I was afraid would happen, Jill, you put me in a thoroughly embarrassing position.'

"Not nearly as embarrassing as if you'd let him in!' she said with a laugh.

'What does that mean?'

'Oh—nothing.'

I felt the blood begin to flow burningly into my face.

'Jill, you weren't—you didn't—'

She shot me a wary glance. 'Oh, come on, Christy, grow up!'

A wave of sickness washed over me. 'Do you mean to tell me you've been—

'Well, for God's sake what did you think we were doing? Sitting side by side on the sofa playing noughts and crosses?'

'I certainly didn't realise you'd turned my house into a lovenest!' I said chokingly. 'God, what a fool I've been! You told me you wanted to talk—'

'That, my love, was a euphemism.'

'But suppose I'd come down? I might well have done—'

'I know. It was quite nerve-racking at times, I can tell you, listening to your footsteps up there.'

I stared at her helplessly. 'And you told me it was for David's sake! Have you any idea how cheap you've made me feel, seeming to condone—that?'

'Sometimes, Christy,' said my sister with asperity, 'you sound like a mid-Victorian governess!'

I only half heard her. 'If Nicholas ever finds out—'

'Nicholas?' She stared at me and gave a short laugh. 'Haven't you got your priorities wrong, love?'

I said again, 'But you said you only wanted to sort things out.'

'Well, we've certainly done that!'

'It's just as well,' I said stiffly, 'because that was the last time.'

Swiftly she changed tactics. 'Oh, now look, love, I don't blame you for being annoyed—I suppose it was a bit much. But—well, we just couldn't help ourselves.'

'I played right into your hands, didn't I?' I said bitterly. 'How you must both have laughed!'

'No, it wasn't like that at all. We hadn't meant it to happen, honestly.' She leant forward earnestly. 'But I love him, Christy, and

142

he loves me.'

'And that makes everything all right?'

'Oh, I know you don't approve of me, you and Father never did. You're right, I *am* a spoilt, selfish little bitch, but look at it my way. I never knew what love was till I met Barry. Does that shock you, when I've been married for nine years? It's true, all the same. And now that I've found someone who's so—so wonderful, I can't let him go! Surely you can see that? Life's too short not to grab at everything you can get. Not a very noble principle, I dare say, but it happens to be mine.'

'So you grabbed for Barry, and now he's in it as deeply as you are. I hope you're proud of yourself.'

Her cheeks flushed. 'I don't have to stand for a lecture from you!'

'No, and I don't have to give in to you. You and Barry are not coming here again, Jill, and that's final.'

'If only Mr Almighty Blair hadn't turned up, you wouldn't have been any the wiser. What did he want, anyway?'

'To discuss a design he wants doing. Now if you'll excuse me, I've a lot of work to do.'

I'd had just about as much as I could take of Jill for the moment, and in any case I wanted to lose no time in finishing all the work I was engaged on at the moment so as to leave myself free for Nicholas's design.

143

At the door she turned back. 'There's nothing I can say to make you reconsider?'

'Nothing whatsoever.'

'Okay. Well, thanks. It was fun while it lasted!' On which flippant note she flounced out of the room.

I put my head in my hands, trying to shut out the picture of them together downstairs while Nicholas and I stood at the front gate. What a blind, credible fool I'd been! Well, they'd have to find another haystack for their romps. I bitterly regretted giving in to Jill's pleas in the first place.

The rest of the week passed without incident. I worked extremely long hours and was glad of the concentration it demanded. I didn't want to think of Jill and Barry and I daren't give myself up to the luxury of remembering Nicholas's kisses. In any case, the harder I worked, the sooner I'd be free for him and could discover just how much the balance of our relationship had changed.

On the Friday, Michael phoned. 'Christy, I am still seeing you tomorrow?'

'Yes, of course.'

'When Blair was so damned possessive—'

'He didn't mean to be. We just didn't want to lose the threads of what we were discussing.'

He hesitated and I was afraid he would press the point, but in the end all he said was, 'I'll call for you at seven, then.'

That Saturday night was not a success. To

my concern, I found myself becoming increasingly irritated by Michael's reproachful eyes and heavy silences. After the rapier thrust and parry of Nicholas's company it was heavy going indeed. Unwillingly, I remembered that Jill had felt the same way about David.

'There was something I'd intended to say to you this evening,' he said at last, 'but somehow the atmosphere doesn't seem too conducive to it.' He paused, but I made no comment.

'The crux of the matter is this. The manager of our branch in Cirencester is retiring soon and Bill wants me to take it over personally. It's been losing business this last couple of years.'

'That should be quite a challenge, then.'

'Yes. But it would mean leaving Biddleton.'

'Oh?'

'Come with me, Christy. As my wife. Before you say anything—' he caught hold of my hands, 'just listen. I hadn't intended to rush you, though I think you know my own mind was made up a long time ago. This move would make a lot of things easier for us. For one thing, you wouldn't be moving into Anne's house. We could choose one together, furnish it from scratch if you like, and sell the other stuff. It would be like a new start for both of us.'

'Michael.'

'Please, sweetheart, don't tell me you don't know. That's always been the answer, hasn't it? I think we've got to the stage where you do know, and just want to avoid hurting me. I can take it if I have to, but I must know one way or the other. Now.'

I said with difficulty, 'I'm being selfish, I know. I'm so fond of you, Michael, but—'

"'But.'" He sat back, releasing my hands. 'That's the word I was afraid of. All right, you may not be wildly in love with me, but we're not headstrong teenagers, either of us. I'm sure we could have a very happy life together.'

There was a long silence. Then he said flatly, 'You don't agree.'

'I—just don't think it would be enough. I'm afraid I'm rather an all-or-nothing person.'

'And it's "nothing"?'

'Couldn't we, to coin a phrase, be just good friends?'

He smiled ruefully. 'I would find it difficult to be platonic with you, my dear. Never mind, it can't be helped. I never really thought I had a chance, anyway.'

I said quietly, 'When do you go?'

'It doesn't have to be till after Christmas, but in the circumstances I think I'll make it as soon as possible.'

'Don't make me feel I'm driving you away. After all, you were my very first friend in Biddleton.'

'You have plenty more now.' He sighed. 'Liz will be disappointed. She took quite a fancy to you.'

Having tacitly relinquished any claim, I was conscious of a feeling of loss. I had already alienated Jill this week, now I was losing Michael. And my position with Nicholas was far too complex to define. I pictured it as a giant pair of scales, constantly tipping too far first one way and then the other, while all my hopes for the future hung precariously in the balance.

Michael broke in on my musings. 'If you should ever change your mind—'

Gratefully I squeezed his hand. It was all the comfort I could offer.

'I'll see you before I go, anyway.'

'Of course.'

All of a sudden we had nothing left to say to each other, and I think it was a relief to both of us when we parted.

I worked steadily all through Sunday, deliberately not going to church, because I didn't want to have to meet Nicholas surrounded by other people. I saw the boys trudging up the High Street with a couple of masters in attendance, and later Nicholas's car with the Temples in it. By mid-afternoon I had finished the last design on my books and wrapped it up for posting the next day. I was ready to start working for Nicholas, and the realisation that I had a legitimate reason to seek him out filled me with a churning excitement.

At eleven o'clock the next morning I took

my parcels to the post office and then drove slowly on down the hill and out on the road to Manor House. As I turned up the drive, I could hear clear young voices coming through the open windows—obviously a singing lesson was in progress. It was, of course, quite possible that Nicholas himself would be involved in teaching at this time, but that was a chance I had to take.

With my fingers mentally crossed, I went up the steps and rang the bell. Through the glass door, I saw a young woman who was crossing the hall, hesitate and come to open it.

'Good morning, I wonder if Mr Blair could see me for a few minutes?'

'Have you an appointment?'

'Er—no, I'm afraid not.'

'Are you a parent?'

'No.'

'I see. Well, perhaps you'd like to come in and I'll find out whether he's free. He doesn't usually see anyone without an appointment.'

I followed her across the hall to her office at the back. She pulled the internal phone towards her.

'Could I have your name, please?'

'Christina Drew.'

She pressed the buzzer and a moment later I heard Nicholas's brisk 'Yes?'

'There's a Miss Drew to see you, sir.'

There was a pause and I held my breath. Then he said, 'Ask her to come up, will you?'

'Yes, sir.' She stood up. 'Come this way, please.'

She led me down a long corridor with classrooms opening off either side. The sound of singing was louder now. We went up a shallow staircase and halted at the door at the top. The secretary knocked on it.

'Come in.'

She opened the door. 'Miss Drew to see you, sir.'

'Thank you.'

She stood to one side to let me pass and closed the door quietly behind her.

Across the room Nicholas rose slowly from behind his desk.

'Hello, Christy. This is a surprise!'

'You said you had some books I could borrow, for the frieze.'

'Oh. Yes, of course. Would you like to sit down for a minute? I'm not sure where they are.' He lifted his phone. 'Miss Anderson, could you bring another cup of coffee, please?'

I looked round the walls at the various framed group photographs and diplomas. A curtain billowed into the room on a draught from the open window. At the bottom of the drive a car passed on the main road. My coffee arrived. There was an almost tangible tension between us which, in view of our last meeting, was hardly surprising.

At last Nicholas said abruptly, 'I believe I owe you an apology, for the other evening. I'd

149

no right to behave as I did.'

'It's all right,' I said ridiculously. So we were going to skate all round it and pretend it never happened. But there I was mistaken.

'The fact is, I don't know where the hell I am with you.'

My startled eyes flew to his face.

'You say you're going to marry Bannister, but you hardly—'

'No,' I interrupted carefully, and it was hard to speak because my heart seemed to be blocking my throat, 'it was you who said that.'

'But you did say you loved him—'

'No. What I said was that I wouldn't marry a man I didn't love.'

He said with a kind of desperation, 'Don't play games with me, Christy. Not now.'

'I'm only trying to put the record straight.'

He held my eyes for a long moment. 'Let's start again, then. Are you going to marry him?'

'No.'

'Do you love him?'

'No.'

He drew a deep breath. 'Well, that certainly puts a different complexion on things.'

'Does it?'

'You know damn well it does.'

'But if you're going to marry Lydia—'

'Do you really believe that?'

I couldn't answer. After a moment he went on, 'However, unfortunately this is neither the time nor the place—'

'I came,' I reminded him with dignity, 'to collect the books. I'm ready to start now, and I need them.'

'Yes.' He glanced at his watch. 'Hell, I've got a class in five minutes.' He went quickly over to some shelves and searched through them. 'Here's one, anyway, to be going on with. And these little guide books are mines of information—there are several of them too.'

I stood up and he loaded them into my arms. 'I'll look for the others as soon as I get a chance and let you have them.' His voice changed. 'We've a hell of a lot to straighten out, haven't we?'

'Yes, we have.'

'The devil of it is that I'm tied up all this week—a series of evening meetings and lectures. It's damnable, but there's nothing I can do about it. Are you free on Saturday?'

'Yes.'

Downstairs a bell clanged and was immediately followed by slamming doors and running footsteps.

'Wait a moment, or you'll get trampled in the rush!'

We stood close together just inside the door, waiting for the noise to die down. Nicholas said softly,

'You know, if I'm not very careful I'm going to make the hell of a fool of myself over you.'

'Likewise, I'm sure!' I said demurely.

He smiled suddenly and bent down,

brushing his lips against mine.

'Till Saturday, then. Goodbye, my love.'

I caught sight of my reflection in one of the glass doors on the way out. I was smiling to myself like an idiot. In the car, I said aloud,

'Oh, darling, darling Nicholas—nothing can go wrong now!'

Which only showed how catastrophically wrong I could be.

CHAPTER TEN

I spent the rest of that day and all the Tuesday browsing through Nicholas's books and jotting down rough sketches as ideas occurred to me. Not that many did, since I kept breaking off my work to go into little daydreams. It was fortunate that such work as I had was connected with Nicholas, or I would not have been able to concentrate on it at all. Several times, as I moved about the house, I paused longingly by the telephone. Saturday seemed an awfully long way away.

I had just finished cooking myself an omelette for my evening meal when the doorbell rang. My only thought as I flew to open it was that Nicholas had somehow managed to get away after all. But it was David who stood outside.

'David, hello! Come in—I was just getting supper.'

He moved slowly into the hall, and something about his appearance struck through my rosy cloud, bringing a sharp, unwelcome memory of the time he had come to tell me about Jill and Barry.

'What is it?' I asked fearfully. 'David, what's happened?'

He turned to face me, lifted his hands and let them fall.

'She's gone,' he said.

'Gone? What do you mean, gone?'

'Cleared out, bag and baggage. No note, no nothing. Apparently she told Ginette to meet both the boys today, and while she was out of the house she must have loaded the cases into the car and taken off.'

'I can't believe it! Surely she wouldn't go without a word to anyone?'

'But she has. Words weren't much good between us now anyway, and she said something last night about your not being sympathetic any more. I wasn't sure what she meant, but apparently she's decided neither of us is any more use to her.'

There was a dull, naked anguish in his eyes and I looked hurriedly away.

'She'll come back—she's sure to.'

He shrugged.

'Come on, I'll get you a drink. Have you eaten?'

'No, I've only just got back from the office. Ginette simply said Jill was out, but when I saw the dressing-table was clear, and all her make-up bottles and perfume gone, I panicked and pulled open drawers and cupboards. Sure enough, most of her stuff had gone, plus the two largest suitcases.'

'She's bound to be in touch, if only about the boys.' Suddenly I stopped dead and spun to face him. 'David, you don't think Barry's gone with her?'

His eyes met mine and from the sick horror in them, I knew that he accepted the idea instantly.

'Oh no!' I said violently, trying to retract the thought before it could take root and grow. Whatever would Nicholas do, if—?

'That must be it,' David was saying heavily. 'Of course—it's the only way it could make sense. Well, if she's got him at last, she'll *never* come back.'

'Perhaps we're wrong. Ring the school and see if he's there.'

'Like hell I will!'

'Then I'll do it.' I picked up the phone in shaking hands.

'Is Mr Fenton there, please?'

'Hold the line a moment and I'll see. Who's calling?'

I bit my lip. 'It's a personal call.'

'Just a minute and I'll find out.'

I waited, each breath requiring a separate effort.

'Hello?'

'Yes?' The phone was slippery in my wet hand.

'I'm afraid he's not available at the moment. There's a lecture in progress in the main hall.'

'But is he there? Is he at the lecture?'

'No one seems to know. It's possible. I'm sorry, I can't help.'

'Thank you.'

I put the phone down and said

mechanically, 'Come and eat. We'll try again later. Jill may have phoned you in the meantime.'

'I doubt it. I told Ginette to phone here straight away if she did, but it's a forlorn hope. God, Christy, where did I go so appallingly wrong? I've never stopped loving her.'

I said slowly, 'You're too nice, David, that's the trouble. You lie down and let her walk all over you.' Not like Nicholas, who retreated rapidly at the first hint of betrayal, who was harsh and implacable when he thought himself rejected. Nicholas! Oh, God, what would this do to him? Suppose the press got hold of it? All his ambitions centred on the unsullied good name of his school. And he was at the wretched lecture too, and I couldn't get hold of him.

I put the rather dried-up omelette on the breakfast table in front of David and started to prepare another.

'I can't eat this.' He stared down at it with loathing.

'You must. You need something inside you.'

'You mentioned a drink earlier. That I could use.'

'Sorry, I forgot. I'll get you one.'

The liquid sloshed over the rim of the glass. Oh, please let it be all right!

I couldn't face the omelette either. Each mouthful was like a wad of cotton wool. I pushed the plate away.

'What can we do?' David asked wretchedly.

He had turned to me automatically, but I was as helpless as he was. I could only shake my head wordlessly. At one time during that ghastly evening, he said expressionlessly, 'I wish I knew what it was she wanted. I'd have given her anything.'

Anything but the things she did want— change, excitement—because those weren't his to give.

For hours it seemed we just sat there, and every now and again I filled his glass. At last— it must have been about eleven he stumbled to his feet.

'I suppose I'd better let you get to bed.'

'It doesn't matter, I won't sleep.'

'I know.'

'David, you will let me know every shred of news you get?'

'Of course. Thanks for putting up with me, Christy. I always come to you, don't I?'

'I wish I could be more help.'

'What in heaven's name shall I tell the boys?'

I had been so enmeshed in fears for Nicholas and David, I hadn't even thought of my nephews.

'Couldn't you just say she's gone away for a holiday?'

'I suppose so. I'd appreciate it if you could come round as often as you can, to keep things as normal as possible. See them to bed, and so

157

on. That is, if it's not asking too much.'

'Of course I will.'

He kissed my cheek. 'Try to get some rest.'

The door closed behind him. I thought numbly, 'At least whatever happens, Nicholas and I can face it together now.' I hoped he would turn to me as David had, but Nicholas wasn't the type to look for a shoulder to cry on. Miserably I switched off the lights and went to bed.

*   *   *

At nine-thirty the next morning, David was at the door again, his face grim.

'I've just had Blair round, demanding to know what was going on.'

'Nicholas?' Oh, why hadn't he come here? 'What did he say?'

'That he couldn't get much out of Fenton's wife, who has apparently gone into the modern equivalent of a decline, but she did say he'd told her he was going off with Jill.'

'Oh, God!'

'He came to see if it was true. I could only say I supposed so—that Jill had said nothing to me and there was no note or anything.'

'Did he—did he mention me?'

David brushed it aside. 'You? No, of course not, why should he? He's got too much on his plate to have time for social niceties. I gather there's a danger of Mrs Fenton losing the baby if she doesn't pull herself together.'

I tried to swallow, but my throat was stretched and dry. 'What else did he say?'

'Not much. My God, I wouldn't like to be Fenton when Blair catches up with him!'

'How did you leave it, then?'

'Just that we'd contact each other if we heard anything and in the meantime do our damndest to keep the whole thing quiet.' He glanced at his watch. 'I must go, I'm late already. You will look in around teatime, won't you?'

'Yes, I'll see you then. Try not to worry.'

But I was unable to take my own advice. I paced the house restlessly all morning.

'Jill Langley,' I said aloud at one point, 'I could wring your neck!'

At lunchtime I could resist the phone no longer.

'I'm sorry, Mr Blair is not taking any calls today.'

I gasped. 'But this is Christina Drew speaking—I think if you told him—'

'I'm sorry, madam, Mr Blair particularly said no calls whatever.'

Dejectedly I hung up. It was a sensible precaution, after all. Heaven knew what rumours might be flying round the village even now. He'd need time to prepare a standard reply to any awkward enquiries. And how, I argued to myself, could he say to that cold-faced secretary of his, 'I won't speak to anyone

159

but Miss Drew?' When he had a moment, he was sure to phone me himself. He must know how I was feeling.

The phone remained obstinately silent all afternoon. Perhaps when school was over—but four o'clock came and went and now it was time to go to David's as I'd promised. I took my pride in my hands and phoned again.

"This is Christina Drew. Is Mr Blair free yet?'

'I'm afraid not, Miss Drew.'

'Then would you please tell him that if he wants to contact me, he can reach me at Biddleton 278?'

'I'll see he gets the message.'

I ran out to the car and drove quickly to Jill's. Or perhaps it wasn't 'Jill's' any more.

'Have there been any phone calls for me?' I asked Ginette immediately.

'No, miss.'

'Hello, Auntie Christy!' Tim appeared in a doorway. 'Mummy's away, did you know?'

'Yes, dear.'

'She didn't tell *us* she was going!'

'Perhaps she thought you'd want to go too, and she knew you couldn't miss school.'

'Mr Fenton can—he's away too.'

I held my breath. 'Oh.'

'Mr Blair took us today. He gave us some awfully hard homework.' He looked up at me hopefully. 'Are you any good at maths, Auntie Christy?'

'I don't think Mr Blair would be interested in my efforts! Come on, you'd better get on with it.'

'I want to watch "Animal Magic".'

'Homework comes first. In you go.' I put an arm round his shoulders and led him into the deserted dining room. 'It's easier to concentrate without the television.'

I listened to his problems, suggested a broad outline which might help, and left him to get on with it while I went to see Mark. And all the time my ears were straining for the phone. Of course, Nicholas had said he was tied up every evening this week, but surely in the circumstances—

David came home and we had our second miserable, silent evening together. I hadn't told the school secretary how long I'd be here. He might phone after the lecture, but he'd hardly want to ring me at David's anyway. As soon as I decently could, I hurried home. It was after ten. There was no ringing to greet me as I crossed the garden, nor had there been by eleven-thirty, when I gave up hope and went to bed.

At half-past one I went through to the kitchen and made myself a cup of cocoa. The familiar little room was strangely alien in the quiet night, with the hands of the clock pointing to an unfamiliar hour. I crouched on the stool where David had sat, clasping the mug and rocking gently backwards and forwards. Outside the window lay the dark garden. Not a star, not a glimmer of moonlight. I was filled with an intolerable ache. Would Saturday never come?

Back in bed I remained wide awake. Out I went again, this time to the living room in search of my favourite Jane Austen. Nicholas's book lay on the coffee table where I had left it that afternoon. Clutching the novel, I went back to bed.

It must have been well past three when I fell suddenly into deep, dreamless sleep, and I awoke to the clatter of the letter box. Almost nine o'clock! I had a quick bath, splashed cold water on my face and dressed hurriedly in case David—or Nicholas?—was preparing to make another early-morning call. Then I went into the hall to collect the letters whose arrival had woken me. But my eyes fastened instead not on them, but on the local paper which lay beside them on the carpet.

'SCANDAL ROCKS PREP SCHOOL' shrieked the black headlines. 'MASTER RUNS AWAY WITH PUPIL'S MOTHER. DESERTED WIFE FACES MISCARRIAGE.'

'Oh, my dear God!' I said in a dry whisper. I didn't even pick it up. I ran into the kitchen for the car keys, out of the back door and across the garden like a creature possessed. My only thought was to get to Nicholas, to be with him during this onslaught. The car bumped crazily down the pitted lane, lurched over the bridge and skidded out on to the main road. I don't remember any more of the journey, just falling out of the car in front of the school.

My headlong flight took me though the swing-doors without bothering about the bell. I couldn't face the superior secretary today, and anyway she would try to stop me seeing him. As though anyone could stop me now!

Fortunately there was no one in the hall; I ran frantically along the corridor I had been shown only three days before, and up the stairs. My tap on the door went unanswered and I pushed it impatiently open. Nicholas was standing across the room with his back to me, his arms along the high mantelshelf and his forehead resting on them. As the door clicked to behind me, he straightened abruptly and in the mirror his eyes met mine.

I said, 'Nicholas! Oh, darling, I've just—' and was halfway across the room before the expression on his face rocked me back on my heels.

'Who let you in?' His voice was unrecognisable. 'I gave instructions—'

'I didn't see anyone. I just came straight up.'

'Then I must ask you to go straight down again.'

His face was like granite. I put out my hands as though to ward off a blow.

'Nicholas, don't—I want to help—'

'Help!' He gave a harsh laugh. 'I've had quite enough of your help, thank you. You

163

realise, I suppose, that my whole career hangs in the balance now? All I've ever cared about was this school.' His voice shook momentarily, but he steadied it almost at once. 'I was even fool enough to tell you some of my hopes for it. And in return you and your sister have gone a long way towards destroying everything it stands for.'

I cried distractedly, 'That's not true—you know it isn't! I've done nothing—'

He broke in furiously. 'Nothing? Can you deny you were a party to the whole thing, lending them your house for their meetings, and going to great lengths to keep me out of the way? No wonder you came flying down the path to meet me that day!' The bitter accusation did not completely hide the hurt that lay underneath and I was defenceless against it.

'It wasn't like that at all,' I whispered. 'I tried to stop them, time and again—'

'By giving them the freedom of your house, I suppose. My God, what a fool you made of me! What a bloody fool!'

'Nicholas, be fair!' I pleaded desperately. 'What could I have done? I—'

'You could have told me.'

I stared at him uncomprehendingly. '*Told* you? Come up to you and said, "Please, sir, my sister's having an affair with one of your masters"? For pity's sake—'

'If I'd known about it early enough I could

have put a stop to it. It would never have reached this stage. If you'd had an ounce of feeling for me—' He broke off, his breathing out of control. 'Well, I've learnt my lesson—by God, I have. No one will ever put me in a position like this again.'

I caught hold of his arm, but he shrugged me off.

'I think,' he said whitely, 'you had better go. We've as much scandal as we can cope with for the moment.'

Somehow I managed to propel my wooden feet back down the stairs and out of the building. I was numb, bruised, locked in a kind of nightmare paralysis where movements that should have been instinctive required every ounce of my strength to become effective. The car, at least, moved of its own volition, and I was grateful.

I remember seeing my own face suspended in the driving mirror, teeth clenched, eyes dry and burning. I turned left out of the drive. I couldn't go home and I didn't want to see anybody. This was one of the dark days of my soul, and I must come to terms with it alone.

It was over. Once again, and for the last time, the giant scales had crashed down heavily against me, just when at last they had seemed to be balanced in my favour. There were no ifs and buts this time, not even any room for misunderstanding. He had the facts quite clear, and if what had seemed to me

165

merely weakness appeared to him as an act of total betrayal, there was nothing I could do to change his mind. To his way of thinking, I had let him down, brutally and unforgivably. The old reluctance to come halfway, to relax, which, to please me, he had tried to overcome, had been proved right in full measure. I knew, and I felt that I couldn't bear to know, that at least half of the pain he was facing now was directly attributable to me.

A dry sob rasped my throat. What could I have done? Was there a moment in time at which, if I could turn the clock back, the situation might still have been saved? If I hadn't lent them the house we might have survived. It would still have been a strain, but we could probably have weathered it. I wondered dully how he knew they had been at the cottage. Barry must have told his wife and she had blurted it out with everything else. Nicholas was not to know that to some extent I'd been betrayed myself. In my stupid naïveté I had honestly thought I was helping them to talk things over and perhaps come to the right decision.

The hard knot of misery inside seemed to grow rather than diminish. I thought dully, 'Somehow I've got to learn to live with this.' And that meant leaving Biddleton. There was no other way. It was impossible to avoid bumping into Nicholas as long as I was there, and the village was no longer big enough for both of us. I owed it to *him* to remove myself with the least possible fuss. I must think of a reason to give David—possibly even the truth. No one else was entitled to an explanation; Michael was already going, anyway. Tonight, when I eventually reached home, I would write after a couple of jobs I'd idly noticed in a magazine.

Somewhere around three, I realised that part of the emptiness spreading inside could be put down to the fact that I had had nothing to eat or drink all day. I seemed to have been on an unconscious tour of the Cotswolds, driving through one lovely little village after another and seeing nothing through pain-dulled eyes. I was now somewhere near Nailsworth, according to the last signpost. I drew up at a cafe and went inside.

'Have you any soup?'

'Soup?' The girl stared at me as though I'd asked for caviar. 'Sorry, just afternoon tea.'

'All right, a large toasted teacake with lots of butter and a big pot of tea, please.'

I sat at a window table. There were plastic flowers stuck in a meat paste jar. Surely the pain couldn't last at this pitch indefinitely. The hot, sweet tea was an atom of comfort. I could only grasp at any such atoms as came my way. In the meantime, I would have to go automatically through each day doing what was required of me. And the first of these duties would fall due about four o'clock, when

167

I was expected at David's. For the first time, I wondered what effect the newspaper had had on him.

If I had hoped to keep my misery secret, it proved futile. David was too much on the same wavelength not to notice the change in me, though I tried to hide it.

'What is it, Christy? Have you heard from Jill?'

'No, it's not that.'

'What's happened, then? The shock of seeing the paper? It was diabolical, but I'd managed to condition myself to expect it. It didn't come as much of a surprise, merely one more blow below the belt.'

I said in a low voice, 'David, I have a confession to make. You won't like it. I only hope you won't feel I betrayed you too much.'

Quietly and calmly I told him of Jill's persuasion and my uneasy compliance. When I had finished, I raised a haggard face to his, bracing myself for his reaction.

'Don't blame yourself too much, Christy. If it hadn't been there, it would have been somewhere else. I don't think honestly that anything could have stopped them.'

'You're more understanding than Nicholas,' I said bitterly.

'Nicholas? Blair? You keep bringing him into it.' His eyes sharpened. 'Has there been something I've missed?'

'We were beginning to fall in love,' I said

flatly. 'After a lot of ups and downs it was just beginning to come right.'

'Then this had to happen. Poor Christy! I'd no idea, but I've been so wrapped up in my own misery I've been blind to everything else. He blames you?'

'He certainly does. He thinks I should have told him and he could have tackled Barry.'

'You couldn't have done that,' said David seriously, and I threw him a glance of deep affection.

'Thank you, that's what I've been trying to convince myself. David, I'll have to go away. You do see that, don't you?'

He nodded heavily. 'Of course. So shall I. Tim will have to be taken away anyway, I can't risk the other boys sniggering at him, not now it's been in the papers. It's half-term next week anyway. I'll give Blair—' he smiled crookedly—'sorry, Nicholas, a ring and let him know.'

'He's not receiving calls.'

'He'll receive mine,' said David grimly.

'Where will you go?'

'To my parents, initially. I'll leave the boys with them and they can go to the village school for the rest of term, until everything gets a bit clearer. I'll have to come back, of course, for work, and to arrange to sell the house.'

'Oh, David, it's so lovely.'

'Even if she did come back there would be too many bitter memories here. Whatever happens we need a fresh start.' His glance flickered in my direction.

'I imagine the usual half-term speech will be a bit of an ordeal this time.'

I hadn't thought of that. One more blow to be rained on Nicholas's defenceless head.

'Look, Christy, Tim can't go back to school tomorrow. I'm taking the day off and we're driving straight down to Dorset. Will you come with us?'

'Oh, David, I'd love to! It would be wonderful to get away for a few days.'

'You can stay there as long as you like, but of course I'll have to come back on Monday.'

'Bless you for thinking of it. Well, I didn't get much sleep last night, so I'll go home now and put a few things into a case. What time will you call for me?'

'About ten. Try to sleep.'

When I pushed open the front door of the cottage, the paper was still lying where I'd first seen it twelve eventful hours before. I picked it up without looking at it, carried it straight through to the kitchen and dropped it in the rubbish bin. With it went all the hopes and dreams of the last few months. How did the song go? 'Pick yourself up, dust yourself off and start all over again.' God willing, I would do just that.

CHAPTER ELEVEN

That breather in Dorset was a life-saver. I don't know how much David had told his parents, but they were gentle and sympathetic and didn't seem to hold it against me for being Jill's sister. We rode and picked apples and collected chestnuts and tried to pretend that all was well. I remember thinking bleakly, 'So Saturday has come at last!' But far from bringing us together, Nicholas and I were irretrievably apart. Had there ever been a longer week? And next Saturday would be half-term, when he would have to stand alone on his platform and face the curious, disapproving, possibly even hostile eyes of the parents.

Tim was curious at his sudden removal from Manor House, but not unduly worried about it. He had made no mention of the boys passing comment on Thursday morning-perhaps they had left home before the paper had been opened. David's prompt action had saved him being exposed to them the following day. Mark, calmer and more placid as always, was perfectly content to change schools in mid-term. To him, his grandparents' home was synonymous with holidays, and to be able to be there during school as well more than made up for the friends he'd left behind in Biddleton.

171

Only David and I, exchanging glances over their heads, had to face the thought of the inevitable return, for however brief a duration.

'I'll come with you tomorrow,' I said on the Sunday evening.

'There's no need to, surely?'

'I've had time to collect myself and I'm grateful, but there's some work I must get on with and I want to write after a couple of jobs. Also,' I smiled across at him, 'it might help if I'm there. I'd be a buffer between you and all the well-meaning people you really don't want to face yet.'

Although David protested, I insisted that he should drop me in Gloucester and go straight to the office. I waited for the bus, closing ears and eyes to the memories that awaited me round every corner—Nicholas in the car outside the art shop—in the café—at the cinema.

I pulled my case on to the bus and settled back for the journey to Biddleton. It was a glorious October day and the trees were a dozen shades of red, gold and brown. The wonderful stone seemed to soak up the mellow sunlight and glow even more penetratingly. Yet despite the beauty, the sadness of autumn was there too, the lingering approach of the death of the year.

My eyes turned longingly to the familiar gateway of Manor House, to the solid front of the Shipton Court Hotel, and so to the Market Square, the duckpond and the sloping village street. It felt like home, but it wouldn't be for much longer.

I left the bus half way up the High Street and went slowly up the path of Kimble's Cottage. The breather was over and life was waiting to be faced again.

One of the unsolved problems was what to do about Nicholas's frieze. I had made several rough sketches, but the last week had not been conducive to work and now I couldn't bear even to think about it. I gathered his books together and put them out of sight behind one of the living room chairs. Later, I would parcel them up and hand them in at the school. In the meantime, there were jobs to write after.

Nobody phoned and nobody called. I had dinner with David each night and avoided everyone else. I was even self-conscious about doing the household shopping, imagining sympathetic glances when none probably existed. It was another endless week.

'You're coming back to Dorset tomorrow, aren't you?' David asked on the Thursday evening.

'I don't think so, thanks. Not this weekend.'

'Why ever not? Surely you don't want to stay here alone?'

I didn't look at him. 'I rather think I'll go along to the school for Nicholas's speech.'

'Lord, I'd forgotten that. Do you want me to come with you?'

'No, it's all right. People won't recognize

me, while they would you.'

'Why do you want to go?'

'I don't really know. Obviously there's nothing I can do to help him, even if he'd let me, but it will at least be one friendly aura. I can't explain it, I just want to be there. I— couldn't bear not to know what happened.'

'Poor Christy,' David said gently, 'I'm more sorry than I can say that this has all rebounded on to you.'

'I'll survive. You go off to Dorset and give my love to the boys. I'll probably come with you next weekend.'

The weight of apprehension increased all day Friday. Once I almost phoned David to ask him to wait for me to meet him in Gloucester after all, but the realisation that the waiting must be ten times worse for Nicholas helped me to stick to my resolve.

Accordingly on the Saturday afternoon I set off yet again for Manor House, parked the car carefully in a position that would ensure a quick getaway, and merged with a group of people going through the doors. The hall was filling rapidly, and there was still twenty minutes before Nicholas was due to speak. Obviously the entire neighbourhood wanted a look at him under stress. I chose a seat right at the back, partly hidden behind a pillar. There was a buzz of excited conversation, and it didn't take much to know what the subject of it was. I sat with my hands tightly folded in my lap and kept my eyes down.

'Personally, I can't think what all the fuss is about!' remarked a fruity voice behind me. 'Now, if the chap had run off with the boy's *father*, the cat *would* be among the pigeons!'

'Oh, George, really!'

'Well, it's damned hard on Blair, he's a first-class chap.'

'Do you think it will have any lasting effect?' someone else asked.

'Difficult to say, at this stage. It *shouldn't*, but it's hard to tell how people will react. Prep schools, after all, are one of the last bastions of the British Empire.'

'You mean that although we're forced to accept the laxity that prevails generally, we still expect rigid standards to be maintained here?'

'That's it exactly.'

A voice above me said, 'Are these seats taken?'

I shook my head. I could feel the blood pulsing in my temples in slow, measured beats. The row rapidly filled up beside me. People were already standing at the back of the hall. Vultures! I thought savagely. It was two o'clock. An expectant rustle ran round the hall, followed by total silence. In the midst of it, Nicholas walked on to the platform and took up his position behind the table.

What happened next was entirely unprecedented. In the far corner someone started to clap, and within a few seconds a

175

storm of applause swept over us and as one man the entire auditorium rose to its feet. As a mark of solidarity it was without parallel. I knew the tears were pouring down my face. I wondered how Nicholas felt. At last he raised his hand smilingly. The clapping died away and everyone sat down.

'Ladies and gentlemen, I can't tell you how grateful I am for your confidence and support. The last two weeks have not been easy, but you may rest assured that everything is being done and will continue to be done to keep the wheels turning smoothly. Apart from that, we can only close our ranks and wait for the publicity to die down.

'I never made a long speech on these occasions, as you know, but this will be even shorter than usual. The school is, as always, open to your inspection and interest. I would just like to add that it is a great comfort to me personally to know that I have so many friends and well-wishers among you. Thank you.'

The clapping broke out again. Someone called, 'Three cheers for the headmaster!' and in the ensuing bedlam I made my escape. I could take no more. Silently I apologised to my companions for underestimating them. Nicholas had not, of course, been in need of my support. Obviously he never would be.

As I ran down the front steps the ringing strains of 'For he's a jolly good fellow' reached me. They were certainly having the whole shooting match. The stupid tears continued to pour down my face, a natural reaction, I suppose, to the suspense and sudden overwhelming relief. I turned blindly towards the car and cannoned into someone who had just come round the corner of the house. It was Valerie Temple.

'Christy! What on earth—? What's the matter?'

I shook my head helplessly and started to run again, but she caught my arm.

'Listen, my girl, you're coming back with me. You're not fit to drive in that condition.'

'I'm all right.'

'I say you're not. Now come along. We'll have the house to ourselves, Robert's on duty.'

I hadn't the strength to argue, so I let her lead me to the little house where we'd all had such a happy evening before things started to pile up against us. I was ashamed of my uncontrolled tears and making valiant efforts to stem them. We went through to the kitchen and I sat at the table while she filled the kettle and took down cups and saucers.

'I don't know why you're doing this,' I said dully. 'You could hardly bring yourself to speak to me at the Golf Club dance.'

She flushed. 'I'm sorry if I was rude.'

'Whatever made you behave like that?'

'I'd no right to. I'm sorry.'

'It's no use just keeping on saying you're sorry. I want to know why.'

She turned to face me, holding the teapot in both hands.

'I just couldn't forgive what you'd done to Nicholas.'

I stared at her in astonishment, the tears drying on my face. 'I? What I'd done to him?'

'Dropping him for Michael Bannister the minute his back was turned. If you'd seen what it did to him— But it wasn't really anything to do with me, and I'd no right to let you see how I felt.'

I said slowly, 'How do you mean, dropping him?'

'Well, you did, didn't you? That evening you were here together, Robert and I couldn't get over the change in him, and you—well, it certainly gave the impression of being mutual. But at the sale you were very careful to let me know how thick you were with Liz—which, of course, meant Michael. And the next thing was that Nicholas arrived home a good ten days earlier than expected and came straight round here asking if I knew where you were. He said he'd tried to phone you dozens of times and could never reach you. So I told him you seemed to be spending all your time with Michael.'

'Just a minute.' I felt I was being slowly torn apart. 'Nicholas phoned me? From Ireland?'

'Yes. He was in a fine state when he came round here—'

'And you told him I'd been with Michael all

178

the time?'

Val stared at me. 'Well, hadn't you? At the sale—'

'You may remember I had just heard Lydia declaring how "poor darling Nick" was enjoying his fishing holiday. You said you'd heard from him too, but I hadn't had so much as a line. It suddenly looked as though I'd been building up my hopes without any foundation at all. So I furiously back-pedalled, so that you wouldn't know what a fool I'd made of myself, and although I'd spent the last ten days avoiding Michael and'—my voice shook—'not answering the phone because I couldn't face seeing him, I seized Liz's invitation with both hands.'

The kettle whistled shrilly. Val said numbly, 'You mean you *were* fond of him after all?'

'Was, am, and always will be.'

'Oh, Christy!' Her hands went to her cheeks.

I said flatly, 'For heaven's sake turn that kettle off.'

She moved awkwardly and poured the boiling water into the teapot. Her voice was shaking more than mine.

'Whatever can I do, to make it up to you?'

'Nothing,' I said sharply. 'It's too late now. We'd just about got over that, anyway, when this last thing broke, and this has finished it once and for all.'

'It's certainly gone pretty deep. *Did* you let

179

them use your house?'

Wearily I tried to explain, but she was only partly listening.

'Well, whatever's happened since, at least I can put things right about Michael.'

'Don't you dare! Nothing you say now will make any difference. Don't blame yourself too much, Val, this last thing was nothing to do with you anyway. I don't want him to think—to know,' I corrected myself ruefully, 'that I've been crying into my tea about it. It would only embarrass him.'

'Then will you go to him, now, when everyone's gone?'

I jerked back. 'Are you mad?'

'Christy, this thing's tearing him apart and the Barry and Jill bit is only part of it. He loves you—'

I shook my head.

'But he does! I know!'

'Then he can come and tell me so.'

She said with exasperation, 'You're as stubborn and stiff-necked as he is!'

'Maybe, but I'm certainly not going to crawl to him again. He threw me out once and that's quite enough, I can tell you.'

'Threw you out? When?'

'I went straight to him, as soon as I saw the paper, and was sent off with a flea in my ear.'

'What did he say?'

'That if I'd had any feeling for him, etc., etc. All right, I was stupid and short-sighted and I didn't work out all the possible consequences, but damn it, Val, that's all. I'd have given anything to stop him being hurt.'

'Did you tell him all that?'

'I didn't get the chance,' I said bitterly. 'He told me he had enough scandal to cope with already and I'd better go. So I went.'

'Yet you came today.'

'Yes. Were you there?'

'I'd just left when I bumped into you. It was—wonderful, wasn't it?'

I nodded and took a quick sip of tea before the tears could start again.

'Don't you think that if I—?'

'Val, if you breathe one word of all this to Nicholas, I shall never forgive you!'

'But *why*, Christy?'

'I've told you. Because there's nothing left now and I don't want to put him in the position of having to tell me so. Oh, it might have been just blossoming at one time—I think it was, especially after what you've told me about his phoning from Ireland. That explains a lot. But whatever there was, he bitterly regrets it now and he's managed to stamp it out completely. You've got to promise me—promise—that you won't do anything at all.'

I held her eye steadily and at last she sighed and looked away.

'Oh, all right, I promise. But it seems such a stupid waste. If he just settles for Lydia after all this, I shall go mad!'

'Perhaps that's what he really wants. No deep emotional involvement—a charming hostess at his side and everything under control. And let's face it, he could do a lot worse.'

'I can't make you change your mind?'

'Not a hope. Thanks for the tea. You were right, I did need it. I'd better go now, I don't want to be here when Robert gets back.'

'I really am terribly sorry I messed it all up. You see, my first allegiance was to Nicholas. I've known him for years, and quite suddenly I felt I didn't know you at all. You do understand, don't you?'

'Yes, I understand, it doesn't matter now, anyway.'

I took a quick look in the mirror of my compact and was relieved that my eyes weren't too red. I powdered my nose and, feeling reasonably presentable, left Val and went down the drive to the car. As it happened I didn't meet anyone anyway. I was glad to have made my peace with Val, but I placed not the slightest importance on her assessment of how Nicholas felt. I didn't dare to.

CHAPTER TWELVE

David phoned when he reached the office on the Monday.

'How did the speech go?'

'A standing ovation, no less.'

'Well, that's a relief all round. It would have been too bad if they'd taken it out on him.'

'How were the boys?'

'Fine. They seem to be getting along without us very well.'

That Monday I also had a reply to one of my letters about a job. They were interested in my qualifications and experience and would like me to go for an interview, taking some samples of my work. I should have felt jubilant, but I didn't.

The week dragged by, and as promised I went with David to Dorset the next weekend. It seemed as though life could plod on in this pattern indefinitely, but actually things were moving beneath the surface. For one thing, David had put his house up for sale, though as yet I had made no move to do anything about mine. It was such a pathetically short time since I had so delightedly bought it.

Another development greeted our return. Val phoned to let me know that Diana Fenton had lost her baby. I wondered whether I should go to see her, but decided it might well do rather more harm than good. It was quite probable that she, and no doubt Nicholas as well, held me partly to blame for this too. I sent a sheaf of flowers with a conventional message, and a guilty feeling of having taken the easy way out.

One day during that week I went to London for my interview. It was with a firm of consultant designers and seemed a very interesting job, designing labels and packages for a lot of the leading food firms. They were obviously impressed with the samples I showed them, and promised to write within a few days, when they had finished interviewing applicants. I had the feeling that the job was as good as mine, but still I could raise no spark of enthusiasm.

The London stores were full of Christmas gifts. It would certainly be a very different Christmas this year from the gentle celebrations Father and I had enjoyed at Bournemouth. We would probably go to the farm, I thought dully, if the weather allowed.

Sitting in the train going home I was aware of an insidious melancholy which was fast becoming habitual. I gave myself a severe dressing-down. It was time to snap out of it. I had spent the last eight or nine years with eyes for no one but David. I had no intention of wasting the next nine pining for Nicholas. And the only way to put him completely out of mind was to get away from Biddleton. My mind circled back to Jill and I wondered if she was happy now, having ruined two marriages and possibly the chance of a third. Was Barry Fenton really worth all that?

The phone rang early the next morning: David's voice, crisp and urgent:

'Christy, can you come round straight away? Jill's here.'

'Jill!'

'She arrived yesterday. I tried to phone you, then remembered you'd gone to London.'

'How is she?'

'I don't know. I can't get through to her at all. Please come as soon as you can.'

He met me in the hall less than fifteen minutes later.

'She's in bed,' he said briefly.

'Is she ill?'

'God knows.'

I ran up the stairs, tapped on the door and went in. Jill lay listlessly under the covers, slow tears tracing their way down her cheeks. As usual, she looked quite exquisite. I surveyed her across the room.

'Well, this is a surprise.'

'Hello, Christy.'

'What made you change your mind?'

'I didn't, Barry did. As soon as he heard about the baby.' Her eyes fastened on mine in a dull kind of appeal. 'She'd have lost it anyway, sooner or later. It was obvious.'

'But Barry doesn't believe that.'

185

'No, he couldn't see it at all. He insisted on taking the full blame. But it wasn't only that. I think I knew after the first three days that it wasn't going to work. At first it was wonderful—just what we'd dreamed about.' Her voice rocked. 'We were together every minute and there was nobody who knew us to see or care.'

She moved her head sharply, her hand going across her eyes.

'God, Christy, I love him so much. I just don't want to go on living without him.'

'We can do without that kind of talk,' I said briskly. 'You've caused quite enough upheaval without starting to hint at suicide, and I might as well tell you that you'll get little sympathy from me.'

She half-smiled. 'I guessed as much. All right, lecture away, I haven't the power to stop you.'

'I'm not going to lecture, but neither am I going to put up with any of your vapours. You're going to snap out of it, but fast, and you can start straight away by getting up and having a bath. Ginette's left, as you know, and I'm certainly not going to spend my time running up and down stairs with trays when there's nothing wrong with you.'

'Nothing wrong!'

'Nothing more than a bit of heart-ache and self-pity. We all have those from time to time, but we don't take to our beds swooning.'

'It's all very well for you—you don't know how I feel.'

'As a matter of fact I know only too well. I've been through quite a lot myself, thanks to you and your escapades.'

'You have? How do you mean?'

'I mean—' I met her eye squarely—'that I'm very much in love with Nicholas Blair.' I heard her gasp but went on: 'And I think he was in love with me. Was. He's not going to forgive me for pandering to you and Barry and letting you use the cottage, instead of reporting the matter to him. So don't keep on telling me I don't know how you feel,' I finished in a kind of choking rush.

The impact of my bombshell had dried Jill's tears.

'You and Mr Blair?'

'I wish you'd stop calling him that!' I said waspishly. 'It makes him sound about ninety.'

'But, Christy, I'd no idea—'

'Would it have made any difference if you had? You didn't consider David or Diana Fenton, so why should you have considered me? Anyway, recriminations don't help now. Come on, I'll run your bath.'

David was hovering on the landing, his eyes anxious.

'Go to work,' I told him brusquely. 'She's all right. I'll stay till you get back, if you're worried about her disappearing again.'

'Thanks, Christy.'

He looked into the bedroom. 'Goodbye, Jill, I'll be back about six-thirty as usual.'

He made no move to go across to her. For the first time, I wondered whether in fact he would be prepared to take her back.

'Stay with me,' Jill said as I prepared to go downstairs. I perched on the linen basket. 'You know David's put the house up for sale?'

'He'd no option, had he?'

'No, I see that.' She tested the water with her toe. 'I have made a mess of things, haven't I?'

'You certainly have.'

'The dreadful thing is that I would do it again.' She lay back in the water and closed her eyes. 'Christy, I'm terribly sorry about you and—and Nicholas.'

'So am I.'

'It was a rotten trick we played on you, I see that. Three and a half weeks, that's all we had. All this upheaval for three and a half weeks. But it was worth it.'

'I'm glad you're satisfied,' I said crisply. 'What did you say to David when you came back?'

'Nothing much. Just that it was over.'

'Is he going to take you back?'

Her eyes flew open. Quite obviously, the alternative had never entered her head.

'Well, is he? I'm hanged if I would, in his position. You drop everything at a moment's notice and rush off with no thought of him and the boys. Then, when Barry leaves you, you crawl back to David, quite sure he'll be only too glad to pick up the pieces. It may surprise you to know that he has his pride, even though you never made any allowances for it.'

'You don't think he should have me back?' Her voice was uncertain.

'I think he should be allowed time to make his own decision.'

'He's had three and a half weeks.'

'But it's never the same until it actually happens. It's easy to say, "I wouldn't let her in the house!" until he sees you. On the other hand, it's equally easy to say, "I'd have her back any day!" and then find out he felt differently when you actually arrived.'

She soaped herself thoughtfully. 'You're not going to let me off lightly, are you?'

'Someone has to give it you straight from the shoulder. Father would if he were here. David really isn't in a position to, in this instance. But he's matured a lot since you went, Jill. I don't think you'll be able to ride rough-shod over him any more.'

My opinion seemed justified when David returned that night.

'Christy, would it inconvenience you very much to move in here for a few days? Just till we get things sorted out?'

I was aware of Jill's stillness.

'Well, I don't know. Jill doesn't need looking after, you know.'

'That's not quite what I meant.'

'He meant,' Jill said shortly, 'that he wants a witness who can testify if need be in a divorce court. By the way, he spent last night in the boys' room. There are to be no unnecessary complications—right, David?'

He met her eyes calmly. 'Right.'

I said awkwardly, 'Couldn't she go to the farm?'

'I don't think that would be a very good idea just at the moment.'

'Meaning I'm not fit to associate with my sons?'

'Not in this highly emotional state, no. So far we've managed to protect them from most of the unpleasantness.'

'Unpleasantness?'

David said heavily, 'What do you suppose Tim's class-mates would have made of his mother running off with Mr Fenton?'

She paled. Incredibly, that aspect just hadn't occurred to her. I wondered exasperatedly if anyone could be more self-centred than she was.

'Do they know?' she asked in a low voice.

'No. Which is why they can never come back here. They might have to know later, of course. We'll see.'

This was certainly a new David, calm, determined and clear-sighted. I looked at him with respect.

After a moment, Jill said tonelessly, 'I'm

190

sorry I hurt you, David.'

'I can live with it.'

'Can you live with me?'

'I don't know, Jill, I'm waiting to find out. It's not a particularly pleasant feeling to be your wife's cast-off. Christy, if you will come I'll run you back now for you to pack a few things. It'll be simpler than taking your car.'

When we were out of the house, I said bluntly, 'Are you serious, or are you just trying to frighten her?'

'I'm serious about not being sure what I want. I still love her, God knows, but one thing's sure. We're not going to start again on the old footing. I was a fool to put up with it before—no wonder she despised me. I'm not going to stand any more of her tempers and tantrums.'

'Good for you,' I said quietly. 'She needs very firm handling and no sympathy.'

'I assure you sympathy is the last thing I shall offer her!' He added soberly, 'I wonder how the other reunion is going.'

We were silent as we walked up the path to the cottage. 'I suppose Barry'll have to leave the school,' I said.

'I was under the impression he'd already left it.'

'I don't envy him having to face Nicholas, let alone his wife. You know, David, he must have been completely infatuated to have thrown away everything like that. I remember telling

Jill at one time that he wouldn't do it. I was wrong.'

'Infatuation is the effect Jill has on people. I think that's what it's been with me all these years. Not any longer, though. Love is the most she can expect from me in the future.'

'It would be enough for most people,' I said unhappily.

David went alone to Dorset that weekend, leaving Jill and me behind. He did not intend to tell the boys of her return until they had made more definite plans. The house was under offer now, and it looked as though there would be no obstacle to a quick sale.

Over breakfast on the Saturday morning, Jill said meditatively, 'You were right about David changing. If he'd been like this all along, I wouldn't have had to look for anyone else.'

'It was you who started it, wasn't it?'

'With Barry? Yes.'

'He's younger than you, surely?'

'Only a couple of years. I certainly wasn't cradle-snatching. Oh, he'd given me a lot of those bold, undressing glances of his, but I knew damn well he did it to everyone. The other mothers used to laugh about it. I thought he was very attractive, but I really only first took him up on it for fun, to call his bluff. It all happened very slowly, over a long period of time. Then I gradually found that I was making excuses to call at the school, looking out for him in church, and so on—and I realised he was doing the same.'

'A pity you hadn't the sense to stop it then.'

'I was bored—I told you. I could have stopped it at that stage, you were right—I simply didn't want to. It added a lot of spice to what had become a rather monotonous life to know that an attractive man was interested in you. Mind you, I'd no idea what we were unleashing. My ultimate aim was only a few kisses in the back of a car.' She paused, making patterns with her knife in the marmalade on her plate.

'The trouble was that at the first kiss there was an almighty flare-up that took us both by surprise. Some freak chemistry, perhaps, I don't know. I think we were both rather frightened, but from then on we were just— swept away by it.' She shuddered.

'And has it burned itself out now?'

'I don't know. As long as I don't see him I can keep it under control. But if he came to me now and said he'd left his wife for good?'

'Yes?'

She turned her head towards me, a blank expression on her face.

'I was going to say I'd go with him like a shot.'

'Well?'

'Quite suddenly, I'm not so sure that I would. It wasn't a pleasant sensation, this obsessive longing all the time.'

'You'd be safer with David?' I asked drily.

'No,' she said consideringly, 'I don't know that I'd be safe with David any more. Not to the extent of being able to do whatever I liked and he would accept it. I have a feeling that if he decides I can stay, it will be on his own terms.'

It was a surprisingly humble speech for my beautiful, selfish sister. I decided privately that David had a very good idea of what he was doing.

When he came back on the Sunday night, she was still subdued, quietly welcoming. I decided they needed to talk by themselves, and retired to bed with a book. I could hear the murmur of their voices downstairs for a very long time after I had turned out the light.

Jill broke all precedents the next morning by coming to my room with a cup of tea.

'Christy, I think it's going to be all right. We really covered some ground last night. We're going to have to work at it, both of us, and David certainly won't come more than halfway to meet me, but I think we can do it.'

I held out my hand. 'I'm so glad, Jillie.'

'He still has his week of autumn holiday left. We're going away somewhere by ourselves— we'll leave the boys where they are. And if all goes well, when we come home we'll look for a new house, somewhere over the other side of Gloucester.'

'That sounds a marvellous idea.'

Her eyes clouded. 'I just wish that you—'

'Never mind that.'

'But it seems so unfair. Barry and I were the guilty ones, and we've both been forgiven and taken back. You and Nicholas were the innocent bystanders and you're the ones who are now suffering the most.'

'It couldn't have been much of a love anyway,' I said with an effort, 'since it disintegrated at the first test. Don't worry about me, just behave yourself from now on. David won't stand for any more nonsense.'

'I know,' she said happily, and left me to drink my tea.

CHAPTER THIRTEEN

I went home that afternoon. Despite Jill's polite protests, I knew I was no longer wanted or needed, which just about wrapped everything up as far as I was concerned. The trouble was, I wasn't wanted or needed by anyone else either. After years of looking after Father, months of trying to cheer David and weeks of supporting Jill, I had come to an end of my usefulness. It was a frightening thought.

The next morning I received a letter from the design consultants offering me the job. That settled it. I put the letter in my bag and went straight down the hill to Selkirk and Bannister. Michael had already gone, but Bill Selkirk was friendly and helpful. He obviously assumed that I was going because Jill and David were. So Kimble's Cottage was back on the market. I felt almost as though I were offering a child for sale.

I still hadn't written back accepting the job by Saturday. I was having to fight an overpowering lethargy. Everything was too much trouble. I couldn't be bothered to start on the new designs awaiting my attention, I couldn't be bothered to do any house-work. A quick flick of the duster and a whizz round with the vacuum was all I'd managed all week.

I stood moodily at the cooker watching the

lamb chop I'd bought for my lunch frizzling gently, the creamy fat starting to brown. And I jumped when the doorbell rang imperiously through the house. I lowered the gas and went to answer it.

Nicholas stood in the porch. The sight of him after all this time was like a physical blow, but pride came to my rescue. It hadn't been pleasant remembering, in the early hours of so many mornings, that I had rushed to be with him in his hour of need and been curtly shown the door.

I said steadily, 'I suppose you've come for your books. I have them ready for you.'

'I ran into Bill Selkirk at the Falcon just now. He told me you've put the cottage on the market. Why?'

'Because I'm leaving, of course.'

'Leaving?'

'Yes. David and Jill are going, as you probably know, so there's nothing to keep me here. And I've been offered an extremely good job in London.'

He stared at me. 'But you're not seriously thinking of going?'

'On the contrary, I'm quite serious and I am going. Now if you'll excuse me, I've a chop under the grill.'

I made to close the door, but he caught hold of it. I turned and walked away from him down the hall to the kitchen. After a moment he followed me. It was the first time he had been

197

inside the cottage.

He stood in the doorway while I turned the chop and put a tomato on the rack beside it. At last he said, 'So there's nothing left?'

'There never was much, was there?'

'Christy, I know I said some terrible things to you that day, but have you any idea what I was going through?'

'Of course, that was why I went straight to you. But you made it very clear you didn't want me.'

'I hardly knew what I was saying, and the thought that you of all people had helped them—'

'Oh, I know,' I said wearily. 'Don't let's go through it all again. I was weak and stupid and completely taken in, but I still don't think that made me a traitor.'

'Of course it didn't. I just had to lash out at someone—'

'And I was there. Quite. But as I don't intend to make a career of being a whipping boy, I won't be there should the need arise again.'

'I don't blame you for being bitter, I behaved abominably, but after all, we've weathered the storm now. Won't you give me another chance?'

I was thankful he couldn't see my face, or know how near I was to running into his arms. But there were things that had to be said if I was to be left with any self-respect at all. I had learnt more from David than I'd realised.

'Please, Christy?'

'That's not quite what you mean, is it? I'm the one to be given another chance. Now that all the sound and fury has died down, you lift your finger and I immediately come running. But I'm afraid it's not going to be like that. You weathered the storm of the crisis in your career, but we didn't weather ours. In fact we sank without trace at the first hint of trouble.'

I wasn't sure how much longer I could keep this up. 'I don't mean to be rude, but is that all? Because my lunch is ready and I'm hungry. I can't offer you any, I only bought one.'

'Please go ahead. I'm not hungry anyway.'

I hesitated, but he was leaning against the doorway with arms folded and showed no signs of going. I put up the leaf, sat down, and, feeling slightly ridiculous, started to eat my chop. It was a wonder that I managed to swallow it.

After a moment he said in a hard voice, 'I suppose you're pretty pleased with yourself.'

'Not particularly, why?'

'You've got the upper hand now, haven't you? A job lined up, and all the rest of it.'

'My dear Nicholas, it might come as a surprise to know that I did not engineer the whole thing merely to annoy you.'

'I notice I'm only your dear Nicholas when you're most irritated with me.'

'As you say.'

'Christy, will you stop eating that damn chop and look at me?'

'Well?'

'You may not believe this, but I've spent most of the last four weeks trying to pluck up courage to come and apologise.'

'You're right,' I said calmly, 'I don't believe it.'

He pushed himself away from the doorpost, his face hard.

'You can't say I didn't try.'

'But you haven't apologised, even now.'

He said stiffly, 'I'm very sorry for speaking to you the way I did. Will you please forgive me?'

'All right, you're forgiven. Now may I finish my lunch?'

My resolve almost faltered at the expression on his face.

'And that's all?'

'What did you expect? I'm afraid I'm rather tired of having to switch my feelings on and off like a tap. It's too wearing. I've accepted your apology, so at least we can part amicably. I'll get your books for you.'

I moved past him into the hall and retrieved them from the corner of the living room. He didn't say a word as I put them into his hands.

'I'm sorry I can't do the frieze, but I'm sure your new art mistress will be able to.'

I was very careful to avoid meeting his eyes as I opened the front door for him.

'Goodbye, Nicholas. I hope all goes well for you.'

He was gone, and I stood in the hall shaking uncontrollably. I had done it. I had salvaged my pride, but at what price? He had apologised and asked for one more chance. I couldn't believe that I hadn't gone straight to him—perhaps he couldn't either. But another chance for what? That miserable swaying backwards and forwards from hope to despair? He had never said that he loved me.

But he might have done, I thought, panic-stricken. If I'd gone to him this time, he might have done. If I never saw him again I would certainly only have myself to blame. Time was fast running out.

During the afternoon, there were three telephone calls. Each time I answered with my heart in my mouth, and each time it was someone wanting to come and view the cottage. My nerves were in shreds. I desperately wished I could turn the clock back to when I had opened the door to Nicholas. If I hadn't been so unbending—it couldn't have been easy for him in the first place. I had made it impossible. I had lashed out at him as he had at me, wanting to hurt. He wouldn't risk going through it again, any more than I would. Val's voice said in my head, 'You're as stiff-necked as he is.'

As the thought came into my mind, the telephone rang again, and it was Val herself.

'Christy, we were wondering if you'd like to come and have Sunday lunch with us tomorrow? Your sister's away, isn't she?'

'I'd love to, Val. I—don't think I'll be at church. Will it be all right if I come about twelve-thirty?'

'That'll be fine. We'll look forward to seeing you.'

I wondered dully if she had seen Nicholas since lunchtime, if she knew that the reason I wouldn't be at church was because they always went in his car. Perhaps he had written me off completely by now and was at this moment having dinner with Lydia.

I stood in the hall twisting my hands together, trying to remember everything that had been said between us, and with each repetition my own attitude seemed more and more suicidal. Was it really worth all this, just to avoid being taken for granted? Yet it wasn't only that which had been in my mind, it had been a kind of insurance for the future. I could see just where Jill and David's marriage had floundered. It was the shock of suddenly not being sure of him which had belatedly made Jill realise David's worth.

Bill Selkirk's information about the cottage must have come as rather a shock to Nicholas. He would have thought I was only waiting for him to apologise for everything to be all right again. There was no doubt at all that he had expected to be given that chance he asked for.

If he had only said he loved me—

I was very glad to have the prospect of Val and Robert's company to help me through what would have been another miserable day. It was Robert who opened the door to me at twelve-thirty the next day.

'Hello, Christy, I'm so glad you could come.'

I hadn't seen him to speak to since the night of the dinner party, and I was slightly self-conscious in his company. Knowing how close he was to Nicholas, I wondered just how much he knew of what had happened between us. He himself gave no sign of embarrassment, and kept Val and me amused throughout the meal with classroom anecdotes, until gradually I relaxed. Whatever happened, I was glad that Nicholas had friends like the Temples.

It was a cold, dank November day, with the sun never really penetrating the thick grey sky. There was a log fire in the sitting room, and after lunch Robert switched on the record-player.

'I don't know if you're a Sinatra fan, but we've quite a collection of his. See if there are any you'd like to hear. I'll just go and give Val a hand to bring in the coffee.'

I sat back on my heels, the firelight warm on my face, and leafed through the brightly coloured record sleeves. Behind me, the door opened.

I said, 'Have you got my favourite—the one about saying something stupid like "I love you"?'

Some quality in the pause that followed my words made me turn sharply. Nicholas was standing inside the doorway looking down at me. The wave of intense relief that washed over me left me feeling dizzy. Perhaps it wasn't too late after all.

'I—thought it was Robert,' I faltered.

'I know. Christy, I just have to talk to you. I realise I may be making a nuisance of myself, and I give you my word that I shan't force myself on you again after today.'

I said unsteadily, 'What do you want to say?'

He smiled a little. 'Possibly "something stupid".'

My heart lurched, but he was going on, 'But not here. This is my last chance and I can't risk any interruptions. Will you come out in the car with me? I know it's not exactly the day for a joyride, but at least the heater works.'

I stood up slowly. 'I'll get my coat. I hope Val—'

'I've had a word with her.'

He held the door open and helped me into my coat. In silence we walked out of the Temples' house and round to the main school building. Nicholas' car was in the drive. I huddled myself into my thick coat and pulled the fur collar up to my ears. After the blazing fire at Val's there was a distinct drop in temperature, though I would have gone to the North Pole with Nicholas had he asked me. In continuing silence we drove down to the gate and turned left on the main road, away from Biddleton. After a few minutes he turned the car off the road and stopped. I rubbed a clear patch on the steamy window and again my heart gave one of those queer, painful little jerks. This was the spot where we'd shared lunch that day in August.

Nicholas said quietly, 'I thought perhaps if we came back here, we could try to blot out everything that has happened since. The number of times I've thought, "If only I hadn't gone to Ireland the very next day." Would it have made any difference, if I hadn't?'

'All the difference in the world, I should think.'

'Darling, what went wrong?' I don't think he realised he had said the endearment. 'I knew, that day, that I was in love with you, though it seemed rather soon to say anything. All the same, I thought I had paved the way when—when we said goodnight.'

'Yes,' I said through dry lips.

He turned to look at me. For the first time it registered that he was pale and there were dark shadows under his eyes. A tide of almost unbearable tenderness washed over me, but he was speaking again.

'What went wrong, Christy?'

'All I knew was that the next time we met, you hadn't a civil word to say to me.'

'But before that? I tried to phone you—'

'So Val said.'

'—Day after day, but I could never get a reply. Where on earth were you?'

'Walking in the rain. I don't know why, I just couldn't bear to stay in.'

'The evenings too?'

'I didn't get back till late. I usually had a meal out and sometimes went to the cinema. I—think I was just filling in time till you got back. I did hear the phone once or twice, but I thought it was Michael, so I didn't answer it.'

He was watching me intently. 'So you weren't with him?'

'Of course not,' I said raggedly. 'I was doing my best to avoid him.'

'That wasn't what I gathered from Val. When I couldn't stand it any longer I packed up and came home. I went round to ask if she'd seen you and she said she thought you'd been spending most of your time with the Bannisters.'

I was lacing my fingers tightly together. They were very cold.

'That was the impression I tried to give her, yes. It was—a kind of self-defence.'

'I don't understand.'

'We went to a bring and buy sale. Lydia was there, telling everyone how you were enjoying your holiday—'

'Oh, God,' he said softly.

'I didn't know, of course, that you'd been trying to phone me. I just thought I must have

206

put far too much importance on what had happened, and I didn't want Val to know what a fool I'd been. So when Liz asked me for dinner, I seized the invitation with both hands.'

He said abruptly, 'Let's get out and walk.'

He opened the door and the cold air swathed about our legs. He reached for my hand and held it tightly. The grass was thick with mist and our shoes were soon soaked. We walked down the hollow where I'd set up my easel and up the slope through the woods. The trees were bare now, lifting skeletal arms to the sky, and the leaves, wet and rank-smelling, clogged the path.

I broke the long silence by saying desperately, 'Why on earth didn't you send me a postcard, anyway, when you'd sent one to Lydia and Val?'

'Because,' he answered softly, 'what I wanted to say to you couldn't be put on a postcard. Then, of course, when I got home, I thought I'd lost you completely.' He gave a short laugh. 'Even so, you'll have noticed that I couldn't keep away from you. It wasn't pure chance that I happened to be driving past when you were at the bus stop, you know.'

We had come out by the rock, but it was too cold and wet to sit on. I remembered the desolation of my last solitary visit here in the rain, and wondered if it had in some way foreshadowed today.

'You're not really going, are you?' His voice made me jump.

'There didn't seem much point in staying.'

'Because of me?'

'Of course because of you.'

'Yet when I came to see you yesterday you were so—distant and implacable I was convinced you could feel nothing for me at all.'

'But you came again today.'

'I had to,' he said simply.

I kept my eyes on the colourless landscape, and I wasn't sure whether the blurring was in my eyes or the mists of the valley.

'I know now,' I said with difficulty, 'that I'd no right to take such a fantastic gamble. But, Nicholas, I was so afraid of being taken for granted, like David.'

'Taken for granted? That's rich! I've never had the slightest idea of how you felt. I can't speak for David, or Jill's treatment of him, but I don't think there's much danger of your ever being a doormat for anyone! But darling, I *have* to be sure of you, otherwise I'd go out of my mind. That's been the trouble all these months. It's not a sign of weakness, you know, to let someone know you love them.'

He seemed to be waiting for me to speak, but I was incapable of it. After a moment he said, 'I've been all kinds of a fool, haven't I? I thought I was pretty self-sufficient and I've discovered I'm not at all. I thought the school would always matter to me more than anything, and I was wrong there too. All I know now is that nothing is worth while without you. What I'm really trying to say is that I love you—and that must be the understatement of the year!'

He turned to me at last, and he must have read my answer in my face.

'I love you, my darling, for want of a more emphatic phrase, with every single—'

We both moved at the same time, and the rest of the sentence was lost for ever. I think we were both acutely aware of how nearly we had missed each other and there was a kind of desperation in that first kiss. When we finally moved shakily apart, smiling at each other a little shyly, the sun hung like a blood orange on the rim of the hill and the swirling mists in the valley below were tinged with rose. We turned, and, with our arms about each other, walked slowly back through the shadowed wood.

'You won't let the cottage go, will you?' he said at one point. 'It would be a lovely retreat at weekends. For that matter you'd probably find it easier to work there during the week too, without all the distractions of bells and games and whistles and pounding feet!' He stopped suddenly. 'Darling, what about that London job?'

I laughed. 'I should think I've missed it by now. I never replied to their offer.'

'Thank God for that! How would a

209

Christmas honeymoon in the Alps appeal?'

'It sounds wonderful, but I don't care where we are.'

'In that case we'll go to Bognor!'

'Nicholas—'

'Yes, my love?'

'I must have Jill and David at the wedding.'

'Of course. Don't worry, sweetheart, I won't snarl at her. Just them and the Temples.'

We had reached the car again. 'And speaking of the Temples,' I murmured, 'I haven't thanked them for my lunch!'

Nicholas grinned. 'Perhaps they can be persuaded to give us tea too. I'm sure it will be a great relief to them to know you're going to take me off their hands. Christy—' he paused in the act of opening the car door. 'Darling, you are sure, aren't you? No doubts at all?'

'I'm sure, Nicholas.' I smiled, and repeated what they often said in the village. 'As sure as God's in Gloucestershire!'

The last of the sunset was fading from the sky as Nicholas turned the car back in the direction of Biddleton.